To Pam

Best Wishes

Robin

21st September
'06

HOLLYWOOD ENDING

BY
ROBIN GREGG

First published in Great Britain in 2006.

Published by Pacific Press International
1A Hugh Street
London
SW1V 1QG

Cover Design: Debra de Villiers

ISBN 0-9552568-0-1

CHAPTER 1

As Peter subsequently related the story: I didn't recognize him at first because I wasn't paying attention. He was notoriously one of a few Hollywood director-producer types who always seemed to find time to party hearty. God knows how because he never appeared to stop working. Anyway, I was occupied trying to explain on the phone to an Italian tourist, using my rusty vocabulary from a high school semester spent in Rome, why he couldn't stay later than the normal checkout time. His room was needed for the next mark, excuse me, customer.

It was only out of the corner of my eye that I noticed a brand new light blue '79 Cadillac sedan glide gently into the parking lot at the side of the motel. Mr Producer came into the lobby looking from side to side as if he wasn't sure of his surroundings and trying to mentally establish if he really wanted to be there at that particular time. Of medium height, overweight and over fifty, wearing a tan coat over an open ended white shirt and light brown slacks, he looked at me straight in the eyes and said "Day Rate, please," at the same time reaching for his wallet.

As soon as a customer utters that phrase, any experienced front desk clerk knows immediately that it is going to be a 'quickie' situation. He leant his bald head, flecked on either side by short grey hair, toward me and said in a conspiratorially low voice, "What's your name, kiddo?"
"Peter," I say and in the same breath, "that'll be fifty dollars, will it be cash or credit card?" An

unnecessary question as he had already put a hundred dollar bill on the desk. He obviously knew the drill because, anticipating my asking for ID, he placed his large paw on my arm.

"Listen, Peter, my name's Jerry, I'm not supposed to be here, you know what I mean?" Winking at me, he fed me the choice bait "I'll give you double to forget the formalities, OK?"

As it happened it was more than OK for me because I was working a scam on the 'dailies' anyway, which one of the other clerks had clued me in on and the less evidence of that the better. I gave him the key for 210 which had been empty since 9 a.m. and at the time of his arrival at 12.20 p.m, I knew that the Lupe, the Colombian maid, had already completed her work on the second floor and was working on the rooms on the ground floor at the side of the building.

This is how the scam worked: a customer who wanted to have a couple of hours maximum use of a room very often would inquire what the "Day Rate" was. Very occasionally, a person would need some time to recover from an exhausting drive or flight into Los Angeles and would need to rest before going about their business.

However, at least ninety per cent of the short time clientele would use the opportunity for the purpose of having sex with another person and not necessarily with the opposite gender. Day rates are a lucrative form of business for savvy motel clerks, especially when they know that the owner of the motel is out of the way and the extra 'pay' was understandably regarded as the top perk of the job. When this type of customer paid by cash which obviously happened a lot of the time, all the sex being extra marital, there would be no record of the transaction unless a receipt was asked for. In the unlikely event of this occurrence, clerks who had done their homework would have made sure that they had a bogus duplicate receipt book available and they would give him or her (yes, we did get women booking into the motel for that reason as well) a page of one of those. Simple really, and the reason that I did it, apart from greed, was that the owner of the place, an unpleasant South Korean by the name of Ky, not only paid his employees minimum wage but had the nerve to insist on charging us if we ever needed one of the rooms for a few hours to catch up on our sleep. So we didn't feel any guilt at all that he was being ripped off of what amounted to thousands of dollars annually because we knew he deserved to be. He was still making a lot of money as the motel was very busy seven days a week.

Every now and then I would insert a cash payment for a day rate into the books to make it look like I was being honest in case Ky was checking up on me. Anyway Mr Producer takes the key and goes to the side door of the motel where he beckons to someone outside who follows him into the lobby and up on the stairs directly across from the front desk. I always make it a habit to take a peep as inconspicuously as possible at the extra 'merchandise' that comes into the motel this way, at least for ID purposes. In fact, the owner told me on my first day that all identification had to be checked for anyone going into any of the rooms but all the clerks knew that this was totally impractical, as it

4

would be impossible to see everyone, especially those entering from the street at the side of the motel. We figured he was just trying to cover his rear end in case of any liability problems and really didn't give it a great deal of thought.

The girl looked very young and was almost certainly underage but I couldn't be sure. After all, the actress Sally Field was still playing the part of a teenager when she was actually more than thirty years old in real life. The girl had mousy blonde hair, was quite tall and certainly had a great figure under a blue blouse and black pants. Only marginally attractive to be honest, I thought, but from my brief glimpse she didn't give me the impression that she was a hooker.

Anyway, away they go and I make a mental note of the time, 12.30, so that I could call the room in two hours to tell him that their time was up and he would have to pay more for an extension if he required it. Friday afternoon is not always a busy time for our motel and I figured with a bit of luck another day rater might come along before business started picking up after 6pm. We had a few vacancies and barring a sudden influx of Japanese tourists on a budget, it promised to be a pretty boring afternoon.

At about twenty minutes to two, Jerry comes down the stairs alone and the first thing I notice is that he is looking very nervous as he approaches me. "Where's the soda machine?" he asks and I gesture to the pool entrance "On the left."
He comes back right away. "Oh the machine doesn't have what I want: I'll go across the street" pointing to the mini-mall. He leaves the building but instead

of crossing the street he disappears round the corner and a few seconds later I hear the sound of a car starting up and backing out of the parking lot. Good, I think to myself, maybe his girlfriend will come down very soon and I can get Lupe to service the room. She doesn't speak English very well and I get the impression that she is working illegally but she is very pleasant and has been friendly to me in the short time I have known her. I give her free sodas and if we're leaving work at about the same time, I walk her to where she catches the bus to her home in East Hollywood. I was just about to page her to service the room when Chester walks in and approaches me with his usual big smile.

Chester is barred from the motel by Ky because not only does he know that he is a pimp but also that he has been warned by Hollywood LAPD that he cannot allow that type of individual on the premises. The reason for this is that, if he does, he will run the risk of having his motel license taken away from him. The California Penal Code, as all employees are informed by the motel's attorney, states quite clearly that 'No business place in the city of Los Angeles shall be used for the purposes of prostitution' amongst other 'deviant practices.' This is in of itself, a problem. Because a guy who is black comes into a motel with a woman looking like she just stepped out of a nightclub show, it doesn't mean that he is a pimp and she is one of his 'working' girls. However, Chester is an exception because not only has he done time for pimping but he has also been arrested twice recently on La Brea Avenue for 'loitering with intent.'

"Hey man, wazzup?" he inquires.

I try to ignore him but he buzzes around me like a bee, trying to get my attention. I come straight to the point.

"You know I can't rent you a room, man. I'll get fired and I don't intend for that to happen."

"It's not for me man, and what's more you don't even know this lady; she's white and she's new in town. I just want you to know she is coming in a few minutes from now and you won't see me again, I swear. Here's a twenty for your trouble."

I see an opportunity here. If Jerry's woman leaves soon, I can double dip on 210 and the whole thing will be over before 5pm when the evening trade starts arriving. So as to show him I'm not an easy mark, I lay down certain conditions.

"Listen to me carefully Chester, this is how it is going to go down and there's no arguing; first of all you have to leave now and don't come back. Secondly, the girl is going to pay me cash no receipt and thirdly, she has to make the bed herself with the sheets I'm going to give the sheets to her because there is somebody in there now who is leaving shortly. Understand?"

"Hey bro, that's cool with me. I'm outta here."

He leaves and I pocket the twenty, feeling very pleased with myself. I look at my watch. Its 2:25 and the girl should be coming down very soon. Hopefully, Jerry would have told her the deal; if she doesn't come down in five minutes, I'll get Lupe to watch the desk and I'll go up there with my master key to deal with it.

It's not exactly unusual to get two dailies running almost together, especially at a motel with the convenient location of La Brea and Sunset. It can be very busy right up to about 9pm during the week, as guys leaving work often have a 'date' before going back to their unsuspecting spouses: as for their partners, some of them actually come from unhappy marriages themselves and are obviously not prostitutes. Late night motel traffic consists to a considerable extent of hookers as well as a few people who are too incapacitated to drive a long way home. Easy access to the Hollywood Freeway to the north of the motel and the Santa Monica freeway to the South down La Brea Avenue, plus the fact that the place is kept in an extremely clean condition, ensures that we get several repeat customers, sometimes even for a week or two at a time.

I'm just about to pick up the desk phone to call the room when I notice the Caddy ease back into the driveway. He'll probably appreciate my calling the room to let the girl know he is on his way back to pick her up. Jerry comes to the desk and while I have the phone to my ear and about to call the room number, he puts his forefinger on the equipment and cuts me off. I'm confused but he says nothing, just shaking his head from side to side. He bends over conspiratorially and whispers into my ear.

"I need a big favor."

"What do you mean?"

"There's a problem and I need your help. I'll call you in half an hour; in the meantime I want you to have this as a present." He presses a bulky white envelope into my hand.

"Don't forget, I'll call you in half an hour for sure."

A sinking feeling goes through my mind and descends all the way to my stomach. This is not

8

good, this is not good at all. Jerry walks out of the door slowly, the way he arrived. While I'm watching him do this, I notice a thirtyish woman come in through the front door and go the pay phone at the opposite end of the lobby. As Jerry drives off for the second time, the woman retraces her steps and comes up to me. She is dressed very casually in jeans and a sweater.

"I'm Chester's friend, Jessica. Can I go up to my room now?"

I have to think very fast, so to give myself time, I stall her.

"Could you hang on just a minute? I'll make sure the room is ready."

I page Lupe and hope that she can come quickly. She doesn't. I decide to risk giving her another room and hope that she'll be in and out quickly before the evening trade starts arriving because it could get busy and I might find myself having only a couple of rooms available.

As luck would have it, I must have miscalculated as only 212 and 217 are free on the second floor and I decide that the latter would be more appropriate as it is around the corner and out of sight. I'll have to make up the bed myself afterwards because Lupe leaves at 5pm and the security guard is invariably late. I think he's illegal too because Ky pays him just enough to get by which means he won't fire him for his perpetual tardiness.

Lupe finally arrives at the desk just as the woman is going up to her room so I ask her to hold the fort while check on 210. Climbing the stairs, I notice that I am absentmindedly holding the sealed envelope that Jerry has given me in my hand, but something else has taken priority in my thoughts. I knock twice on the door. No answer. I put the master key in the lock and push the door open.

The girl is lying naked on the side of the bed on her back with her head on the pillow with her one right foot on the floor. The first thing I notice about her motionless body is that her eyes are open and there is a red mark on her pale skin on the left side of her neck. At first I think she is looking at me and asking me to say something to her before she responds; to begin a dialogue as it were. Although my brain is not functioning very well, I say, "Miss, are you OK?"

She makes no response and I begin to tremble as if confronted by an extremely disturbing situation. An overwhelming force of nature now renders me speechless. Not exactly a misplaced emotion because it suddenly hits me forcefully: She's dead, very dead.

CHAPTER 2

Heart racing, panic settled on my brain like pigeons on tossed breadcrumbs. I behave irrationally, moving around the room trying to figure the best way to deal with the situation. Suddenly, I realize that I'm still holding the brown envelope that Eric had given me some minutes earlier and I absent-mindedly put it into the back pocket of my jeans to be opened later. I spot out of the corner of my eye the strap of a purse hanging out of a half open drawer under the table at the side of the bed. Ignoring the possibility of leaving my fingerprints, I inspect the quilted purse. It is empty except for a small wallet. Curiosity overwhelming me, I open the wallet. It contains two one hundred dollar bills folded neatly, a few coins and half a dozen dollar bills. Great, I think, the police will really be impressed that yet another hooker has met an untimely end in Hollywood. After an extremely brief deliberation, I resist the temptation to remove the money. I've never taken a lie detector test and this is not a good time to find out whether they are effective. The only other article in the wallet is a driver's license. I stare at the face. It is young, attractive and with long light brown hair, substantially differing in its healthiness from the person who arrived in the hotel two short hours ago.

Catherine Mack.

1651, Acacia Drive,

Madison, Wisconsin, 53562.

I see that she is or was twenty two years old. I try to make the connection between the photo and the person lying on her back naked, her eyes staring at me. I find this very difficult and turn away with the sudden realization that I have contaminated the crime scene considerably. I leave the room, closing the door behind me and rush down the stairs trying to compose myself, which I find difficult to do. I put my hand in my pocket to finally inspect the contents of the envelope when my attention is distracted, to my surprise and annoyance, by noticing Chester slipping by Lupe out of the door to the pool area. In my agitated frame of mind, I yell at him.

"Hey, man, what are you doing here? You know you can't do that."

He freezes like a kid who has been caught stealing candy and turns around to face me.

"Oh, sorry man, I was just checking to see if my chick got here yet."

"Don't lie to me, man, you were sneaking in hoping I wouldn't see you."

"Well, that too." He knows I've got him cold and smiles at me.

"This is a very bad time, Chester. I've got a serious problem. You've got to leave now. Anyway, you don't want to be here right now, I promise you." This piques his interest and he's on the verge of asking me to explain, but he sees the angry expression on my face and thinks better of it.

"See you later."

"Make it much later, very much later and I mean it!"

He slinks out of the front door and walks down the street. I watch him turn right at the lights on Sunset. I hope he stays away for good although I seriously doubt that I'm going to be that lucky.

I call 911 to report the death in the room without giving too many details, professing shock. It is said that a man's life flashes before him on his way to the execution chamber and I feel that way now. The main reason I came to Hollywood was to hope to break into the film business and although this is the second movie I've starred in since my arrival two weeks ago, I'm not aware that I'm going to be paid for this one either.

I take the envelope out of my back pocket and inspect it. I see that Jerry has written on the front "Remember, you never saw me." I open it. It is full of the green stuff, all Franklins. I quickly count them and repeat the process just to make sure. It still came to the same amount. Thirty. Three thousand dollars. It looks like I'm going to be paid for this movie after all.

CHAPTER 3

My first instinct is of self preservation. It's amazing what you can think of to say when you've only got a few moments to get it together. But first of all I have to decide where to stash the cash. Obviously not in the safe and leaving it anywhere else in the motel is out of the question. Too late to think of anything else as the black and white was pulling up out front. I stuff the three grand into my jeans and quickly rip up the envelope and throw it into the trash can. Radios crackling, two uniformed officers burst through the front door: one black, one Hispanic, they approach the desk as a team.

"OK. Waddwe got here?" growled one of them. More of a statement than a question. Before I had a chance to respond, the Hispanic officer held up his hand close to my face as if to interrupt me as he barked into his transmitter the location of his considerable presence. I turned to speak to the other officer.

"There's a woman in 210. I think she's dead."

Lupe, who had overheard my 911 call sits in a chair in the lobby, with her face in her hands reciting her rosary, obviously in a state of distress. The second officer briefly glanced at her before rejoining the conversation.

"You think, huh. Did you take her pulse?" I couldn't detect from his manner whether he was being facetious so I played it safe.

"No."

"Did you touch anything?"

"No."

I figured that if my prints came up positive on anything I could say it was by accident when I went into the room. Either way I knew I wasn't responsible and hoped the cops would see it that way too.

"Take us up there," the black officer command. Upstairs in the room, shadows began to fall over the bed as if a metaphorical curtain was descending on another wasted life. One of the officers reached for his radio. "Location Best Inn. 1511 La Brea, just north of Sunset. Jane Doe. Ambulance requested."

As I was coming back down the stairs with the black cop, a plainclothes officer was coming through the front door. Detective Bard was a short unimposing figure in a grey suit and plain black tie with a rapidly receding curly blond hair. Strolling into the lobby nonchalantly almost as if he was checking into a room himself he, however, got down to the business at hand very briskly and in a very professional manner. Although at first he seemed to be non-combative when he introduced himself, as soon as he began to question me I got the distinct impression that he could turn nasty at the drop of a hat.

Succumbing to momentary paranoia, I envisaged myself in custody as a suspect before the evening got much later.

"Okay Lopez, do we have a suspect?"

After being briefed on the situation, he fixed his gaze on me.

"Start from the very beginning; what time did this young lady come in and was she alone or did she have someone with her?"

"Well, it was just after 12.30p.m. and….."

"Are you sure about that?"

"As I was about to say," I thought it would not be a good idea to add 'before you rudely interrupted me' "I know it was that time because I looked at the clock on the wall over there at the same time."

I neglected to mention that the real reason I looked at the clock was because I knew it was going to be a quickie and I wanted to be sure that I knew when her time was up. That would definitely not have gone down very well. "A guy booked in first and she followed five minutes later and asked for a separate key but I refused to give her one because she wouldn't give me any ID."

"Can I see the john's registration?"

Once again I had received a command disguised as a question thrown at me and I decided that there was no point in trying to deceive the detective.

"There isn't any."

"Why not?"

"Because I didn't register him."

"Look sonny, stop playing games with me: a few seconds ago you said you….."

The detective's sentence was interrupted by the sound of yelling from the pool area, growing louder and louder, until the interior door opened and a handcuffed Jessica stumbled into the lobby, still shouting at the top of her voice. She was accompanied by the Hispanic officer who was holding her right arm.

"Shut the fuck up," Bard screamed.

"I didn't do no thing, no thing," said Bard, mimicking her southern drawl.

"What's the deal here, Hernandez?"

16

"I caught her trying to sneak out the back. I think she could be a material witness."

"OK. Take her out to the pool. I need to finish this off and then I'll come and question her. Put the bracelets on her."

"Sure thing."

During this brief interruption, I make a quick calculation. I know that when Ky gets here and one of the officers has already told Bard that he's on the way, my job is history, but at least I know I have a comfortable financial cushion. I think. Fortunately for me, Lupe had been upstairs when Jerry came in the first time and no one else saw him either as far as I know. I make a decision that I know I am going to regret but at the time I have no idea of the massive consequences. Bard turned back to me and comes close in an obviously intimidating manner.

"As I was saying, first you said the guy registered and now you say he didn't. Which is it?"

"I didn't take his details."

"Why not? I presume you know that's against the law. I could bust you for that right now."

"Well, he said he was going to be…"

"Don't give me that bullshit. You thought you could make a little matinee money, didn't you?"

No use, he had me locked up tight.

"Well, yes."

"Describe him."

"He was black. About five eight, five nine with a muscular physique and close cropped hair."

"How old?"

I describe Chester perfectly down to his immaculately pressed khaki pants and brown loafers. I even added his mannerism of regularly blinking his left eye.

"Good, very good. By the way, how long have you been working here?"

"About two weeks. I started working nights but after a couple of days I got moved to this shift when the owner begun using a relative at the later time." I declined to mention that the boy was seventeen years old and was a nephew of Ky's who was on probation for a drug offence.

This was hardly the time to be negative about a fellow worker regardless of his background, besides which I liked him.

"Right, I need you to give your details to one of my officers. Lopez!" he yelled to the officer just outside the lobby. "Take this guy's statement and bring in the girl when you're done. She most definitely could be involved."

He gestured to me, "I don't think you're going to have any customers for a while. We got this place locked down tighter than a drum."

This authoritative statement coincided with the arrival of Ky. A stocky man in his fifties, his face was beaded in sweat, although it was quite chilly outside. He looked as if had run all the way from Koreatown. He was dressed in fashionable sweats and wearing athletic shoes. Looking at him I couldn't make up my mind whether to feel sorry for him or not. He was mean to his employees but he was going to be out at least several hundred dollars tonight due to the police activity and he now stood the risk of having the motel shut down for the foreseeable future.

"What happen? What happen? I hear somebody dead. What happen?" he repeated.

Bard turned his attention to the intruder whom he appeared by his facial expression to hold in considerable disdain.

"I regret to inform you, sir, that your motel has been the scene of a suspected homicide. We both know that this is not the first time that a fatality has occurred at this location. I must tell you that this is not a satisfactory situation."

In the corner of the room Lupe began to sob again. Everybody appeared to ignore her.

"A dead woman has been found in a room upstairs," Bard continued. "Your employee," pointing at me, "cannot provide any evidence of registration by herself or her male companion and I strongly suspect that this person met her death after entering the motel for the purpose of offering sexual services. There is no doubt in my mind that the preliminary report of the medical examiner who is upstairs in the room as we speak will indicate that the cause of death will have been unnatural, to say the least."

Ky's facial expression remained unchanged through all of this. Either he was a better actor than I gave him credit for or he was in shock and I personally preferred the former explanation. He looked at me but said nothing, obviously waiting for a more appropriate opportunity.

"We have an ID on the woman but it's from out of state and we're checking it out right now. I need to get a statement from you." With a wave of the hand, Bard gestured towards the outdoor pool area.

"See the officer out there. I've got to finish up what I'm doing."

As soon as we were alone again Bard resumed his questioning.

"Something perplexes me: If this black guy is who I think he might be, why would he go up to the room with the girl? Also, we found two one hundred dollar bills in her purse. Where would that have come from?"

"I don't know. Maybe she had it on her when she came in."

"You mean from another john?"

"I don't know." I was beginning to sound like a parrot. "Maybe she was going to pay for something later."

"She was going to pay for something later," Bard repeated, as if to imply sarcastically that this was a unlikely scenario. Maybe he wanted me to correct myself and show him that I wasn't giving him the full story. Good idea but there was no way I was going to go along with that. Now he was really giving me the evil eye and I felt certain that not only did he believe that I was lying but that I knew that he had already come to that conclusion.

"Go and see Officer Hernandez. I want your DOB, present address and your statement and we'll almost certainly need you to come down to the station for further questioning."

Ky came back into the lobby while Bard was talking. Approaching the detective, he gestured in my direction "He finished here." Scowling at me, he grunted "Pick up your things. You fired."

CHAPTER 4

The effort of getting on the bus had not been that difficult for Peter. In fact he was glad to get out of Columbus. Circumstances beyond his control had predicated a disappearance from a family scene that had become unbearable. His mother's untimely death from medical malpractice during a botched operation to remove a tumor from her stomach was made even more traumatic by the fact that exactly the same operation had been performed a year previously, obviously with a less than a satisfactory conclusion. The tumor had returned. This time his mother had bled to death after the operation. This tragedy was compounded by his father being completely oblivious to the conniving nature of his secretary at his place of business. A much younger woman who took it upon herself to be the more than a willing shoulder for her employer to lean on at a time of his great personal grief, she had only been working at the company for just over a year at the time of my mother's death. However, she readily replaced the wife with the only remedy for my father's pain and there was absolutely nothing that Peter, the only child, could do about it, as he reconciled himself grimly. He didn't help his cause by not welcoming her gracefully, as his father apparently thought he should, into their much depleted lives and he had to admit that he resented her intrusion into the space that he felt belonged to the two men.

Also, he and his father had grown apart over the years that had passed since he had left high school. He had failed to live up to the aspirations that the older man had planned for his son; without asking him for his input he once admitted that he had visions of Peter becoming a judge. Exactly how he had expected him to rise to this lofty pinnacle was never disclosed and Peter was not entirely convinced that his father had any serious inkling that this position entailed many years of scholarship and application.

No, it was time to move on and though lacking in financial stability, he made the decision to become another emigre from Ohio to Southern California. His decision was strongly influenced by watching on television the bright warm sunshine of the New Year's Day Rose Parade in Pasadena on numerous occasions. So, it was with the princely sum of $157.60 that was left after buying a one way ticket on the Greyhound bus to Los Angeles. Peter joined his fellow drifters and Christmas vacation returnees of limited funds to take the laborious route - is there any other route on Greyhound? - to the Mecca of the movie stars.

He had been promised temporary accommodation in a Hollywood apartment belonging to the girlfriend of a guy he'd roomed with at college and with whom he'd kept in touch. He owed Peter a few favors so the latter saw nothing wrong with this arrangement.

Getting off the bus at Union Station downtown, he made a mental note never to subject himself to this form of travel again as long as he lived. He'd had very little sleep in just under thirty hours of traveling and his back hurt like hell from staying in an upright position for so long in spite of having had several rest stops on the way. He was advised by a stranger to take the city bus to Hollywood Boulevard and Highland Avenue and walk two blocks west to Sycamore, the street that his friend lived on.

Peter had no difficulty finding the right house number on the block which was just as well as his suitcase was starting to get heavy. He rang the front doorbell and waited for a while without a response. He rang again, this time for longer. Still no luck. Peter looked at his watch. It was 4:40 p.m. and the light was fading fast. He decided to walk round to the back of the two story building hoping to find someone there. Unlike most of the houses on the rest of the street, this was a property that had seen better days and looked like a good coat of paint wouldn't do it any harm.

Avoiding a couple of trash cans, Peter tapped on the back window of a room where a light dimly shone. After a few moments, the back door of the house opened inward.

"Hey, buddy, what's up?" asked a muscular guy who looked to be in his early thirties with dark blond hair and who was wearing a white t-shirt and faded blue jeans.

"I'm looking for a friend who I think lives on the second floor; I'm supposed to be staying with him for a few days."

"Come in; I don't think anyone's home right now though."

Peter carried his suitcase up the stairs in the dark. At the top of the stairs he could barely see a light switch. He flicked it and the bulb threw a dull glow down the corridor which ran to the front of the building. He knocked on the apartment door on the left, then on the right. No answer. While Peter was figuring out what to do next, T-shirt's voice called out from downstairs.

"Any luck?"

"No, I guess not."

"Well, why don't you come down here and have a cup of coffee while you wait for your friend to get home."

Peter descended the stairs and went through the door of the apartment where his new acquaintance was standing in the middle of the living room. He noticed immediately that the scene was one of considerable disarray. Boxes half full of clothes and household objects were strewn over the floor. Some electronic equipment including a television set was piled up in one corner of the room.

"Sorry the place is in such a mess, I'm just moving in," T-shirt smiled.

He closed the door and Peter heard the click of a latch. All of a sudden, he didn't like the place he was in but he thought simultaneously that he could have been over-reacting through sheer exhaustion.. He stood his ground with his tote bag still over his shoulder and his suitcase at his feet. T-shirt made no effort to continue speaking but his facial muscles started twitching. Finally he continued.

"I wonder if you could help me," he began and then paused as if to test the reaction to this phrase. "I'm a little tapped out right now and I've got to make just one more delivery from the Valley," jerking a thumb behind him as if his listener would automatically know the area toward which he was gesturing.

"Could you front me some gas money till my girl friend arrives? She'll be here later."

At this moment three separate thoughts were going through Peter's mind. Firstly, how difficult was it going to be to get out of the room, secondly was this a shakedown or was he really just a tad paranoid, and thirdly, what would happen if he told him that he couldn't help him out? He decided rapidly that he would test all three hypotheses by trying to stall.

"Look, man, I just got into town and I don't have any bread but I'm sure that when my friend gets back home I can ask him to help out. I'm expecting him to advance me some bucks myself anyway to get me over the next few days till I get a job."

T-shirt made no immediate response but just kept looking at him. He could almost see him mentally digesting this development. For a full minute he stared in Peter's direction as if at a loss for words and only when the latter bent down to pick up his suitcase did he speak.

"Hey, you know something, buddy?" Obviously, his favorite word of affection. "That's not what I wanted to hear from you. Cut the crap, I know you got money on you."

Before Peter's thought process could allow him to reply, he reached into his trouser pocket, pulled out a switchblade and flicked it open..

"I'm going to cut you, I'm going to cut you. RIGHT NOW!"

T-Shirt had raised his voice a couple of decibels without changing the expression on his face which somehow made him even more menacing. It has been often said that reality bites and Peter suddenly realized in a split second that although he had only just arrived in Hollywood, he was already featuring in a low budget film production. This was not the role that he would have preferred for himself as it was one which could very probably signal the beginning and ending of a meteoric but extremely brief career. However, he had always dreamed of being a successful actor and now fate was giving him the chance of being talented enough to extricate himself from a serious real life situation.

"Don't hurt me man. I'll give you what you want; I won't give you any trouble."

He had about forty dollars in his wallet and the rest stuck down his pants pocket. He took his wallet out of his coat and handed it to T-shirt.

"Here it is; that's all I've got. Take it"

Peter hoped that his captor would be satisfied with that and that the gesture would convince him that he was trying to be as co-operative as possible. After removing the cash together with a driver's license and Social Security card, T-shirt threw the wallet back at Peter who took this to be a positive sign. He would hardly be returning his wallet if he was going to kill him.

Glancing again at his watch, Peter noticed that it was just coming up to 5.30 p.m. Surely, he thought, somebody should be coming home soon. Would he be able to attract their attention and anyway would it be worth the risk? He could try jumping out the window but he reckoned the fall would be about fifteen feet onto concrete and he might do himself a serious injury.

Outside he could hear the traffic intensify with the arrival of the rush hour. So near and yet so far, he thought. T-shirt seemed to read his mind.

"Turn around," he barked, "don't look at me any more."

This order was almost as reassuring as the returning of the wallet because unless he was going to literally cut his throat, it did not appear that he was going to inflict any injury on him.

"I'm going to have to tie you up. Put your hands behind your back."

First the knife, now a piece of rope. It seemed that this guy had been prepared for any eventuality. After he removed the watch from Peter's wrest, the rope was tightened professionally and harshly. Peter got the feeling that he had certainly done this sort of thing before. For a moment, he toyed with the idea of trying to subdue him but just as quickly dismissed this thought from his mind. The man was tall, well-built and looked very fit. Peter was shorter and by now physically as well as mentally exhausted and the only advantage that he would have was the element of surprise. This would be negated by the fact that his adversary had a knife and he had nothing with which to defend himself. He must have put the switch blade back in his pocket because after tying Peter's hands he grabbed his left arm and with his other hand started going through his trouser pockets with the inevitable result.

"Lying to me," he spat out as he discovered the rest of the money.

"I was hoping you'd be satisfied with what I gave you," Peter lamely offered, knowing very well that he wouldn't have been. The last thing that he remembered was T-shirt's right fist coming towards his head and him screaming "WELCOME TO HOLLYWOOD!"

CHAPTER 5

Peter's first impulse after regaining consciousness some time later was to wriggle out of the rope that tied his hands together. Having done this with some difficulty, he then ran his hands over his body to see if any limbs were broken. He was greatly relieved that his arms and legs were OK and although his head hurt, it still seemed to be still attached to the rest of him. Peter had been the victim of a vicious assault and considered himself lucky not to have been seriously injured at the very least by his knife-wielding assailant. Staggering to his feet, he groped in the darkness for a light switch. He found one near the door but the flick up and down produced nothing. He could barely see his few clothes scattered on the floor along with the contents of his tote bag. It was very doubtful that anything of any importance would be missing for the simple reason that there wasn't anything in his few possessions worth taking. Stumbling out of the room into the corridor, he found the light switch on the stairs and back up he went to pound again on what he hoped was his friend's door. Still no answer.

Suddenly, the door across the hall opened half a crack and through the slit he could see the face of an elderly bald man peering at him.

"Stop banging. There's nobody there."

"Do you know what time anybody's coming home?"

"Nobody's coming back, fella; those two got evicted last week."

"Evicted? What do you mean?"

"They didn't pay the rent, at least that's what the landlord told me. Anyway, this whole place has just been sold. I've got to leave myself in three weeks."

"I got mugged downstairs by a guy who said he lived there."

"Really? Too bad. Why don't you call the cops? They'll come in four weeks - if you're lucky." With that encouraging news, he slammed his door.

At the time he most needed some help, it looked as if there wasn't going to be any, Peter reflected despondently. He went back downstairs and gathered up his belongings and threw then into the suitcase, closing the lid. Taking stock of the situation, he realized that it would be difficult to find a place for the night with no contacts and no money. Shutting the door of the apartment and placing a chair under the door handle, he decided to bunk down for the night. If someone tried to get in, he would at least be warned by the noise even if he was asleep on the floor. Peter was by then in a state of complete physical and mental exhaustion. He felt it unlikely that T-shirt would come back and maybe, just maybe, he could get a few hours sleep. He passed out almost immediately and didn't wake up until day-break.

The sun was shining into the room but the atmosphere felt cold to Peter although he could see that the sky was clear. He had not been disturbed although he had no idea how long he'd been asleep because his watch had been taken from him. Gathering his belongings, he emerged onto the street from behind the building, Peter quickly realised it was a good idea to look for some employment. Walking down the street, he was struck by the peacefulness of his surroundings and once he reached Hollywood Boulevard he observed that the main thoroughfare was also quiet with few signs of activity. A clock in the front of a store indicated that it was just after 6.30 a.m.

Any brief thoughts of contacting the police vanished from his mind almost instantly. Would they believe his story? Probably not.

Acting on an impulse, he decided to continue his journey up to what he could see was a residential area. Although lying in an uncomfortable position on the floor all night, he had slept like a log. He tried to ignore the dull pain caused by being assaulted and which was now throbbing through his head as he made his way up the street. He retrieved a half eaten chicken sandwich from his duffel coat and chewed on it hungrily as he came to an intersection. The sign read: La Brea Avenue. To the right, the road wound steadily up toward an extensive mountain range on either side of which were apartment houses which he could see eventually led to what looked like more expensive private homes. Not much point going in that direction, he thought. He turned south toward the blinking lights of what appeared to be an extensive commercial district. After walking on a slightly downhill grade for a couple of blocks, he could see on the left a motel with the sign BEST INN with the middle 'N' un-illuminated like a missing child. He wondered if the proprietor cared; it didn't look like a very high class establishment.

Without having the vaguest idea what he was going to say or do once he got to the front desk, he opened the door and approached the clerk. This

31

individual, whose head was completely bald but did not looked much older than thirty, was bent down over a sheet of paper apparently adding up some figures with the help of what seemed to be an antiquated piece of electronic equipment.

"They used beads at the last place I worked," Peter suddenly blurted out for no particular reason other than it sounded funny. The man, who looked up and looked him over, chuckled at the remark.

"Yeah, we keep asking for new gadgets but the owner has short arms and long pockets, so it's a no go. You looking for a room?"

Before I had a chance to reply, in the negative of course, there was a loud scream followed by the sound of a splash of water reverberating through the air.

"Holy shit," yelled the clerk. That's the second one this week. I got to deal with this."

He leaped out of his chair and vaulted over the counter. Turning to Peter, he blurted out, "You look pretty straight, fella, do me a favor will you? Look after the store for a minute. In case anyone comes, tell them I'll be right back."

And that more or less, leaving out the boring details, is how I managed to convince the owner that I was reliable enough to be trusted with the graveyard shift at The Best Inn.

CHAPTER 6

So, to get back to the present, there was good news and bad news. The good news was that he had $3000 cash but the bad news was that he had lost his job and was at very least a possible suspect in 210's death. Also he had to factor in the probability that Chester would be just stupid enough to get himself arrested and he would be brought in to in to identify him. Bard had taken his statement at the hotel which gave him a surge of optimism that he wouldn't be arrested as an accomplice. He was put in a squad car and driven the eight blocks to Las Palmas to the guest house where Peter rented a matchbox, not out of courtesy but because it was obvious that the detective wanted to make sure that he lived where he said he did. Although this actually was his first confrontation with the cops because it would have been a waste of time reporting the previous assault, it was astonishing how quickly he was able to embrace the police culture of the big city. I've grown up very quickly after getting off that Greyhound bus, Peter thought.

He decided to check out of his room right away as he needed to find another place to live, which would require some legwork. Peter took the money out of his pocket and counted it again in the manner of a person who wasn't sure if it was real. It was real all right. As he was leaving his lodgings, putting it in the motel office safe was not an option. The old lady who passed for a manager he had no problem with, but her son was a different matter. He formed the distinct impression by his body language that the man didn't like him very much. Knowing that if he deposited a considerable sum of cash to be kept on his behalf, this would make him very suspicious as to its origin considering that Peter had said when he first arrived that he did not have a lot of money to pay for a room.

He went back down the stairs, crossed the lobby and went out the front door. The two elderly men who were watching the communal TV (this place wasn't fancy enough to have personal TVs in every room) hardly looked up as he went by down the steps and out on to the street. It was now 11 p.m. and the streets surrounding his humble abode were humming with weekend activity. Peter didn't notice the black limo with tinted windows as it slowly drew up beside him and stopped. The window on the driver's side silently rolled down and a young red haired man dressed in a dark blue suit beckoned with his hand to Peter.

"Get in."

"Excuse me?"

"It's OK. I've been over at the motel where you work. Eric sent me"

"I heard you the first time, you don't have to repeat yourself. And who's Eric? "

He was trying to convey a sense of awareness, an impression of being someone with a hint of intelligence but in fact he had for sometime now realized that, if he was being honest with himself, he would have accepted that that he was completely out of his depth. Hanging uncertainly between the two states of refusing to accept the precarious circumstances in which he had placed himself and the desire to disassociate himself from any of the day's dramatic events, his mental condition had become one of intense internal turmoil. It showed.

"Look, I can tell you have a problem believing I'm your friend. I'll prove it to you by getting Eric on the phone"

The limo continued to cruise alongside Peter as he was walking down to Hollywood Boulevard as if he had to convince him one more time.

"I work for him." Slight pause." Here he is, speak to him yourself."

With this, Redhead stuck a car phone out of the window, very vaguely in Peter's direction as if to say, 'the choice is yours, take the phone and speak – or not – I don't really care'.

Peter deliberated for a couple of seconds. His instincts told him he should walk away and get these people out of his life as quickly as they had entered it. He was a provincial who had come to Los Angeles to get away from a stressful life and try to make a fresh start and the last thing he needed was further complications. Unfortunately, they were already there and he had the sense of impending doom rapidly descending on him. Also there was the small matter of the 30 Franklins, and if it was really not a hoax and Jerry was really on the phone, he needed to reassure him that he would keep quiet about what happened. He became even more confused than ever.

"Yes?" He inquired tentatively into the phone.

"Hey, Peter"

The voice was unmistakable and sounded upbeat.

"Is everything OK?"

Before he gave Peter the chance to reply, he carried on.

"Did the cops give you a hard time?"

Peter decided to play along and see where the conversation took him.

"I thought your name was Jerry"

"Forgive me for that, I was being careful"

"Well, it was pretty tough, I am not sure the detective bought my story."

"What did you tell him?"

Peter went through the sequence of events carefully, omitting any reference to his benefactor's involvement. Redhead was listening and he didn't want to let him in on anything he may not have already have known.

"Listen Peter; I want you to get in the limo and come up and talk to me."

"Now?"

"Yeah, I'm at a party. I want you to come up so I can explain some stuff to you personally."

"I am actually looking for somewhere new to live" Peter responded. I just got fired and I don't want to stay at my address anymore."

"Oh, that's not a problem. I'll take care of that. Trust me. It's only a twenty minute drive at most from here you are now."

"How did you know where I live?"

Eric chuckled.

"I arranged to make sure you were OK, Peter. Don't you think that's the least I should do?"

"I suppose so."

"I'll explain everything. I'll make sure you get back to Hollywood OK."

What did he have to lose; he was up to his neck in trouble and he didn't think it could get much worse in just a few hours. Peter opened the limo door and climbed in the back. Redhead seemed pleased. He smiled, reached back over the seat and shook his hand. Away they went.

"Where are we going?"

"Eric's agent is throwing a party at his house in Beverly Hills. There will be some familiar faces there," Redhead said matter-of-factly as if it was no big deal.

"I don't even know for sure what Eric does for a living"

"He's a film producer. You could say he's pretty famous" Red paused as if giving Peter time to digest this information. "I thought you knew that"

"No, but I've seen his face in magazines a couple of times."

The limo purred up Sunset gradually ascending into an area that consisted of expensive looking houses on both sides of the street. Red remained silent as if preoccupied with his own thoughts and Peter didn't feel comfortable revealing too much of his own state of mind to a complete stranger.

"I'm not really dressed properly for a fancy party"

"Oh, don't worry about that. Dick's parties are very informal. He actually walks around barefoot himself."

They approached an intersection where a large sign on the right stated: Beverly Hills Hotel. Red made a sharp right turn immediately afterwards and began a steeper ascent. Traffic was almost non existent for about a mile although Peter noticed the mansions becoming more opulent the further up they progressed on what according to a sign was BENEDICT CANYON DRIVE. Red made a right turn into a smaller street. Suddenly they found themselves backed up behind three other limousines being waved on by car valets carrying neon stickers in an attempt to speed up the traffic.

One final left turn up a leafy side street and they were there. As he got out, Peter felt like the character in Citizen Kane, a film he had seen as a ten year old boy, who arrives at Xanadu, the home of the protagonist portrayed by Orson Welles. At the gate, an officiously mannered individual was holding a clipboard checking off names on the guest list. Red approached him nonchalantly as if they were old friends.

"This is Peter. He's with me."

Mr. Clipboard's stern face creased into an attempt at a grin which gave Peter the impression it didn't happen very often.

"Yeah, Mr. Dagle said you had a guest. Carry on." He waved the limo up the driveway. Above, Peter could hear the loud babble of conversation and music coming from the house. They were halfway up the driveway when Red's friend yelled out at them "Hey, Red. This guy says he's with you!" We looked back to see a bulky middle aged individual in an ill-fitting brown suit being restrained by Mr. Clipboard's assistant.

"No, he's not with us!" exclaimed Red. Peter's immediate reaction was that it must be a wonderful party if a person would come all the way without an invitation and hope to crash it by pretending to be an invited guest. How little did he know at the time how often this happened in Hollywood.

CHAPTER 7

It is not always easy to see how large a house is at night. Dimensions take on a different perspective in the light of day but it was immediately clear to Peter that the front was so broad that its width was of considerable size. A mock Elizabethan turret in plain white took pride of place at the front of the mansion in the middle of which was a large open door of veneered mahogany. On either side of the front door were large stained glass leaded French windows attached to oak wooden panelling which gradually curved round towards the back of the mansion. Standing at the front of this unusually designed residence, was a tall man with a full shock of white hair who was talking to Jerry who he had to remember was actually named Eric.

"Peter, come on in and meet your host Richard."

Turning to the latter, he remarked, "This is the young man I've been telling you about."

A thought immediately flashed through Peter's mind. He couldn't have gone into detail about today's events, could he? No, that would be so bizarre as to be completely impossible. As quickly as the idea arrived, Peter dismissed it as another moment of total paranoia. It was then that he noticed that, as Red had said, Richard was bare footed.

"I hear you are going to start working for Eric. I have to warn you that he is a slave driver." A brief pause as both men laughed.

"No, I am kidding. He is a great guy who helps me to live the way I do."

Peter couldn't make up his mind whether to be pleased or alarmed that someone else was trying to determine his future without approaching him for his input. Eric seemed to sense his uneasiness and decided on a shift of emphasis in the conversation. As the two men followed Richard into the crowded living room, Eric put his hand on Peter's shoulder and confided, "This is your lucky night; I am going to introduce you to a lovely young lady who is going to have a great future as an actress. In fact I am giving her a part in my next movie."

"Oh really," their host interjected "That's a contradiction isn't it, Eric. I thought you just said she had a great future."

"Very witty, Richard. Sometimes I wonder if you really want to remain my agent."

Peter realized that the two friends were having a hoot scoring points off each other just like a pair of vaudevillians he had seen so many time in old movie musicals.

"Come on young man, lets go meet her."

It was then that Peter realized that Red was no longer with them. His job was done and he had melted away into the huge party throng. Eric took his arm, but instead of joining the crowd, guided him to a corridor which led off the lounge and into a study. He closed the door.

"Tell me what happened."

"Everything?"

"Yes, everything."

Peter started slowly not wishing his memory to fail him. I knew what he really wanted to know, he thought; if he had implicated him in any way. He realized that Eric didn't care about anybody else's problems except his own and after a couple of minutes a feeling of remorse – or was it guilt?, or maybe a combination of both, began to overcome him. For a split second he had the wild impulse of taking the money out of his pocket, throwing it at Eric and bolting out of the house; out of the mess he had found himself in. Then he pulled himself together. What good would that do? He was in deep and there was no turning back. Not only did he know it, but Eric knew that Peter knew it too. He was trapped. The popular expression 'between a rock and a hard place' was hardly sufficient to sum up the situation that he had been thrust into; The only possible mitigation was that he hadn't asked for any of this to happen. He was young and naïve and not for the first time since arriving in Hollywood two weeks previously he had been caught, this time metaphorically, with his pants down.

Peter finished his story. As Eric looked pleased, he decided to take the bull by the horns as he felt he could not be in any more trouble anyway.

"What happened with you and the girl?"

Eric looked as if he had been grossly insulted and his voice hardened.

"Listen, son." This was the first time he addressed Peter in this way. "It was a horrible accident." Eric suddenly grabbed Peter by the collar and pulled him closer. He was an older man but was powerfully built and Peter didn't try to resist.

"You aren't wearing a wire, are you?"

Before he could answer, Eric patted him down. Satisfied, he let go.

"Sorry, but I know how life goes; I just had to make sure."

The thought occurred to Peter that if he had been wearing some electrical device, that could have been his last minute on earth. It was obvious that Eric was possessed of a considerable temper and that could explain the reason for the tragic event earlier that day. Peter decided it would not be a good idea to pursue the subject. Changing gears, he asked "Can I meet that young lady you were talking about earlier?"

Eric's expression softened.

"Why not? Follow me." With that, they plunged back into the gathering.

To say that the huge lounge was inhabited by several instantly recognizable people would have been an understatement of some magnitude. A well known comedian was holding court in one corner, in the middle of an elaborate story as they passed by. Peter overheard a famous veteran actor shaking one of his peers by the hand while saying "I know we've never met but I have always admired your work."

Yes, it was that kind of night. Peter started to overdose mentally on the star power present. Eric brought him back to reality. He took Peter's elbow and pulled him over to a couch where a suave looking man was talking to one of the most attractive young women Peter had ever seen. Looking to be in her early twenties, she had long blonde hair around a classically formed face which curled over her shoulders cascading onto her breasts visible under a tight blue satin dress that appeared to be a size too small. Her companion was casually decked out in an open necked white shirt and grey slacks with crocodile loafers. He looked tanned and

42

fit but his plain features did not indicate leading man stature.

Eric did the introductions somewhat perfunctorily. "Peter, this is Lucy. Lucy is from England and has decided to spend some time with us and I hope she will make it permanent. And this is my partner in crime, I mean my production manager, David Geld."

Peter could tell right away that Lucy had been drinking. Her face was flushed and she was unsteady on her feet when she got up to embrace Eric and shake hands with the young man.

David broke the awkward silence that followed.

"I've been telling Lucy that you'd like to run through some dialogue with her as soon as possible."

Eric chimed in "Good. Good."

Turning to Peter, "Before I forget, here's my card; call me tomorrow morning I need to speak to you about something and may need to see you as well."

"Well, I don't have job anymore so I don't think that is going to be a problem," Peter blurted out as Eric abruptly turned and walked away without a backward glance. No sooner had he said that, than he had second thoughts.

What was Eric trying to say? Was he offering him a job and if so, what was it? Could this be a continuation of the pattern of bribery begun earlier? He was determined to find out as soon as possible.

In the meantime, he directed his attention to Lucy and her companion. Just as he was about to make what he considered to be a flattering remark in her direction, they both got to their feet and left him on his own. Peter sat down on the couch next to where Lucy and David had been sitting and pondered his next move.

A stoutly built woman in her fifties with closely cropped silver hair plonked herself down beside him. She seemed as inappropriately dressed for a swank Hollywood party as he was. She wore a severe tailored black jacket over a mauve shirt with a medium length black skirt and chunky shoes that are often derisorily described as 'sensible'.

"Hi, I'm Tommy. I handle publicity for Eric's production company. Pleased to meet you."

Peter was afraid to ask her exactly what she meant so he played dumb. With her short grey hair she looked more like a school teacher in her outfit than a member of the film industry, but what did he know. Mistaking his silence for politeness, Tommy rattled on.

"I used to go to a lot of these parties but I just got tired of them. Always the same people over and over again and quite frankly I got bored."

She paused as if to observe it he was taking in her monologue and was obviously encouraged by Peter nodding his head up and down slowly as if in sympathy.

She continued. "Eric tells me you're new in town."

"Yes, I've been here only two weeks."

"Two weeks! I don't remember the last time I met somebody who'd only been for such a short time." She laughed loudly in the manner of someone who thought she'd said something extremely funny.

"What did you do before you came here?"

The last thing Peter wanted to do was to be quizzed by a stranger but mindful of the situation in which he had found himself he didn't have much choice. After a brief version of his family history and his decision to follow a new path in his life, he casually mentioned that he had met Eric earlier in the day and that they got on very well together. He prayed that his version did not differ in any material respect to what she had previously been told. It obviously didn't, because she invited him to call her at the number on the business card she pushed into his hand. Having satisfied her curiosity about his respectability, at least for the time being, she departed, most probably, Peter thought, to find another victim.

For the first time since he had left his budget hotel he was alone and he took the opportunity to put everything into perspective. Instead of making his own decisions, his experiences had forced his hand. To put it in John Lennon's words 'Life is what happens when you are busy making other plans.'
He concluded there and then to go along for the ride and see how far this adventure was going to take him. After all he had come to Los Angeles to seek 'fame and fortune' at the age of twentyfour and maybe this was the way that fate had planned it to be. Peter pulled himself to his feet and decided to mingle, well, mingle until he found Lucy again. Maybe they had something in common that could develop into a friendship despite his poverty.

The lounge was more packed than ever as the party had apparently reached its peak. A charismatic individual who had finally won a best actor Oscar after having lost twice previously, as Peter remembered, for much superior performances, was with his wife. He was chatting to a Middle Eastern looking man who was gently reminding him that he hadn't been to his club since having his Academy Award celebration there the year before. Peter suddenly realized that being an avid film buff for a number of years was finally paying off for him. Not only was he recognizing a lot of faces but he was able to connect them to their respective backgrounds as well.

After circling the room a couple of times, he failed to spot Lucy or her companion and decided to escape the smoke and incessant conversation by exiting through the back of the house for some fresh air. A pool, adorned with submerged lights on all sides appeared before him, the base of which was decorated with a mural of a beach and coconut palms, lay to the left. Further on stood a tennis court with overhead lighting surrounded by a wire fence at the far end of which was a closed gate. The net was up invitingly but no one was taking advantage of the opportunity, no doubt too busy yapping away and getting drunk. After all, the opportunity to indulge oneself at a select party was irresistible even for celebrities. He decided to take a stroll on the pathway to the right of the court where he spotted Richard chatting with an older man with a large cigar in his mouth as he passed by. Peter nodded and smiled in their direction.

At the end of the pathway was a flower garden surrounded by bushes which appeared to be part of a landscaping attempt to augment an empty area next to an outside bar. Richard and his companion advanced in this direction. His host beckoned to the young man.

"Peter, would you like a drink?"

Before he had an opportunity to reply, they were interrupted by a long low moan coming from behind the bar area. The bushes on both sides concealed the source. Richard swiftly advanced in the direction of the noise, in order to identify its origin, followed by two very curious companions. They were amazed to find lying on the grass, David and Lucy, 'in flagrante delicto'. He was lying on his back with his pants and trousers pulled down while Lucy was on her knees vigorously performing oral sex on him. David had his eyes closed but his mouth was open and it was from there that the groaning was coming.

Peter looked at Richard not knowing what to say. The latter's face was contorted with rage. It didn't take long for the inevitable outburst.

"DAVID!! What the hell do you think you two are doing?"

At this, David opened his eyes in shocked surprise and pushed Lucy to one side. Simultaneously he pulled up his underpants and trousers, jumping to his feet and zipping up quickly.

"Sorry"

"Sorry!! It's that all you have to say to me?"

By this time an embarrassed Lucy had struggled to her feet and did her best to rearrange her disheveled cocktail dress and straighten her hair. She looked as humiliated as Peter had ever seen anyone and a feeling of pity and sympathy began to sweep over him.

David looked at Richard in silence, knowing that his apology was totally inadequate but was obviously fearful that saying anything more might make a bad situation worse.

"This is disgusting behavior. I invite you to my house and you abuse my hospitality disgracefully. There are children present tonight," waving towards the house, "suppose they had seen this. You are a production executive who presumably knows better. I certainly hope so anyway. I will not tolerate this. You have to leave now and take your girlfriend with you." David tried to say something but Richard abruptly cut him off.

"I don't want to hear your excuses!" he shouted. Pointing to the pathway to the right of the house, "That's the way out!"

To Peter's astonishment, David walked off without even a backward glance to Lucy. She looked miserable and Peter wanted to put his arm around her to comfort her but he knew this would be social suicide. Glancing briefly at Richard, who was standing with his hands on his hips. Lucy trudged away disconsolately and the trio watched her disappear around the side of the house towards the exit.

CHAPTER 8

Acting on impulse, Peter followed the girl around the side of the house keeping her in sight as he walked past some guests who were naturally unaware of the incident. He wasn't sure if she needed his help or even if she deserved it, but something in the callous behavior of her fellow 'culprit' touched a nerve in his gentlemanly instincts and he was also intrigued enough to want to observe what her next move would be.

Lucy walked swiftly towards the gate without a backward glance in the manner of someone who was more than anxious to get away from her surroundings.

Peter caught up with her by the gate. A car valet approached.

"Do you have a ticket?"

"No, I came with someone and I won't be waiting for them."

Peter saw his chance to intervene.

"There's a shuttle taking people down to Sunset Boulevard. I saw it going down when we were coming up here. Can I wait with you until the next one comes?"

Lucy looked at him questioningly. Peter decided to take a gamble.

"Look, I saw what happened. I am not going to judge you and I feel very badly about the way you were treated afterwards."

"Were you with the host? I didn't see you."

"I just happened to be with him at the time. By chance....." His voice tailed off.

"I see."

"I know you probably don't feel like talking to anybody right now but I've had a long day and I want to leave. Do you mind my coming down in the shuttle with you? If it's OK, we can take a cab at Sunset and I can drop you off anywhere you want to go."

"My coat and purse are in my girlfriend's car but I don't dare go back into the party now."

"I don't blame you."

The ride down the hill was taken in silence. It seemed to Peter that Lucy was using the time to recover her composure and he did not wish to indulge in any conversation anyway that would have been inappropriate in the company of fellow passengers. Later, as they drove to Lucy's address in the cab, Peter decided on another gamble.

Without revealing Eric's complicity in the crime, he disclosed to her what had happened in his life in the last 24 hours and how he had ended up at the party. Peter rationalized that, as this strategy gave the impression of confiding in her, she would reciprocate by trusting him and possibly becoming his friend which was is exactly what he wanted to happen. If she was insincere or uninterested, she would surely make it plain immediately and part company with him by leaving him to complete his journey on his own.

Lucy listened intently until they arrived at her place. Peter looked at his watch as if to prompt her into making a decision.

"Why don't you come in? We could have some coffee."

Jokingly, Peter responded, "I would have said my place, but I don't have a place. Just a seedy motel room in Hollywood that I am leaving tomorrow. I was leaving it tonight but events caught up with me."

Inside her apartment, small but clean and tidy, Lucy sat at the kitchen table watching Peter as he drank his coffee.

"Did you say that Eric offered you a job?"

"I'm not sure what he wants from me or what he wants me to do. We didn't get that far. Thank God he gave me his card at the party otherwise I wouldn't be able to get in touch. I need to apologize to him for leaving without saying goodbye."

"Yeah, me too." Lucy laughed.

"Well, I've confessed my sins. It's your turn now."

"Got a couple of hours?"

It was Peter's turn to laugh. "Why not?"

Lucy slowly and meticulously began her adult life story. Literally. She had arrived from New York seven months previously after coming there to visit an American boyfriend she had met as a student in London, while he was on vacation. He had almost immediately promised her his undying love, not to mention the earth the moon and the stars, and she had come over to America to rekindle their relationship. In spite of the misgivings that family more often than not declare in such a situation, Lucy had taken the plunge. She had only been in New York for three days when she realized that she had made a serious error of judgment. Her boyfriend turned out to be a serial womanizer incapable of sustaining an honest emotion for fear that it would die of loneliness.

She contacted a British Airways flight attendant whom she had known in London. Her friend had met a millionaire film investor while attending to his needs in the first class compartment of a Trans-Atlantic flight. Flash forward and she was now living with him at his palatial oceanside residence in Malibu. She offered his waterfront cottage to Lucy as a temporary place to stay until she could get on her feet. Lucy accepted gratefully. After all, she reasoned, as she had come all the way to America, she might as well go across the country to see what life on the other coast had to offer.

The millionaire liked the idea too as it gave his girlfriend someone to spend time with while he was out of town amassing even more wealth and he liked the idea even more when he first laid eyes on Lucy on her arrival at his home. Things went fine for three or four weeks but then while Patricia, for that was her name, was away on a flight, Mr.Big Bucks invited Lucy to a party at a business associate's house in Pacific Palisades. Not for the first time in her life she got rip-roaring drunk. It was probably a reaction to the quiet existence she had been leading in her new life in Malibu. Where she was living was a bit out of the way without a car and while the time with Patricia was enjoyable, especially when being taken around sight seeing, time dragged when she was on her own.

Whatever the circumstances, the sex was unsatisfactory, Mr. B.B. not being the most accomplished lover in the world, but a dangerous precedent had been created. Far more serious for Lucy was the knowledge that she had betrayed her benefactress and her guilt had caused her to be uncharacteristically subdued when Patricia returned from her eight day absence. As she explained to

Peter, it didn't take long for her friend to realize that something had happened and Mr. B.B.'s denial of complicity was not exactly convincing. A frosty chill descended on the young women's friendship and as the situation became daily more intolerable, Lucy found herself homeless again.

Although his motives were hardly altruistic, Mr. B.B. seemed to have a twinge of conscience, and he secretly arranged for Lucy to move into the Brentwood apartment building in which one of his employees resided. He also paid the rent on the apartment for six months in advance. So Lucy moved from being a relationship wrecker to a kept woman which did nothing for her self esteem. During that period she received multiple visits from her sugardaddy presumably while her ex-friend was out of town (Lucy didn't dare ask). In the meantime, she managed to make some friends on social occasions and gradually inserted herself into the loop, commonly known as the party circuit.

Eventually, through contacts, she came to the notice of a casting agent and she was invited to come in and read for some minor parts in television programs. However, whenever it looked as if she was about to be cast in a small role, she ran into the same brick wall: No Work Permit. In order to protect citizens and legal residents, particularly in any over-crowded profession such as the entertainment industry, this was a stipulation that could not legally be the subject of a loophole. In truth, Lucy's visa to stay in the country had expired and technically as well as factually she was in breach of immigration regulations. Added to this, the reality that she was a stunningly beautiful blonde worked against her to a certain extant because the element of jealousy invariably entered the equation. Lucy realized that it was only a matter of time before one of her rivals would stumble on to the fact that she had a legality problem.

Enter David Geld who could only be described as a "hot" producer on a winning streak. He was a regular attendee at Jerry Isenberg's Friday night events on Sunset Plaza Drive north of the Sunset Strip which were held every two months or so. These were get togethers for industry insiders almost all of whom knew each other and were not averse to arriving with eye candy to show off their ability to attract beautiful women regardless of their position in the Hollywood hierarchy.

However, Lucy had come to the party on her own because, as she explained the story, her girlfriend who was invited got sick earlier that day. Being a close friend of Jerry's, she had given Lucy permission to use her name to obtain admission if necessary. As it happened it was a 'walk-in' for her, probably because of her appearance.

In no time at all the bees were buzzing around Lucy. In contrast; David was laid back. He had spotted her but played a cool hand waiting for about half an hour before approaching. She had never heard of him and for some reason this excited his male ego even more as well as convincing him that she wasn't just another Hollywood bimbo who was trying to suck up to him to get work. He was a lot younger than Mr. Big Bucks and seemed to have none of his baggage.

The relationship began that night and developed gradually although Lucy quickly figured out that she wasn't the only 'meat on the tenderizer'. In time, she mentioned her legal problem and David promised to help.

About two weeks later he set up an appointment with an immigration lawyer who put in motion the bureaucracy needed to legitimize her continued presence in the country. The wheels were turning slowly, as the attorney warned her they would, and the situation was still in limbo at the present time.

Peter noticed that after talking for about an hour, Lucy's eyelids were beginning to droop and his reaction was to feel a wave of exhaustion sweep over him as well. It had been an exhausting day, and as he instinctively slumped lower on the divan trying to fight the tiredness which was now extensively overcoming his senses, Lucy bravely tried to carry on between yawns.

"I got very drunk tonight...It's something I'm trying not to make a habit of these days. David was feeling frisky and he said that no one ever came to that area at Richard's parties because it was always so close to the edge of the property. I don't know what I was thinking," she continued lamely.

"You don't have to explain yourself to me, Lucy. I'm not in any position to judge anybody."

"You're so sweet."

"I'm tired. I feel like I've just run a marathon."

Without another word Lucy got up and returned with a blanket. She lifted Peter's feet up onto the divan.

Walking over to her bedroom, she opened the door, turning back to say "Sleep well" and closed the door behind her.

CHAPTER 9

Peter awoke with a start. He looked at his watch. Jesus, he thought, it's nine twenty-five a.m. I must have slept for at least eight hours. Lucy's bedroom door remained closed. She's probably still trying to recover from her disastrous experience, he reckoned. Anyway, he realized that he had to phone Eric as soon as possible, I'm going to need some advice on what to do, he reasoned. Ky owed him a week's salary so he had to go round to pick it up. He didn't think he was going to get a hard time over this as the guy would probably be anxious not to have any more problems.

Peter scribbled a note for Lucy and left it on the kitchen table. He put the phone number of the motel on it hoping that he would hear from her. If he didn't, he could always come round to see her. He definitely didn't want to lose contact. There was something about her that he found intriguing and he felt that they had bonded during the course of their conversation.

The sky was cloudy and rain was threatening as Peter made his way back to his lodgings. After breakfast, he would once again begin the effort to find an apartment. Fortunately, Lucy's place had not been more than ten blocks away, near Fairfax, and it didn't take Peter long to find a pay phone. Wouldn't it be nice, he thought, that one day everybody would be able to communicate by private phones that they would be able to carry around with them and thereby being in constant communication with each other. Peter had read an article to the effect that the technology to create this phenomenon was far advanced and a break through was imminent. Right now, people were dependent on pagers for contact and he made a mental note to obtain one as soon as possible.

"Yes," Eric barked, "Who is this?"

"I apologize for not saying goodbye. Something happened and I helped Lucy to ..."

"I heard what happened," Eric interrupted. "Everyone's talking about it. The Hollywood Reporter is running a story about it on Monday."

"The Hollywood Reporter?"

"Boy, do you have a lot to learn. Listen, Peter, would you do me a favor? Hop in a cab and get over to my office at Paramount at Melrose and Gower as quickly as you can. I'll pay for the cab. I have something very important to discuss with you about the film I've got in production. I can assure you it's very much in your interests to come over."

"I feel dirty. I didn't go home last night. I have to have a shower and change clothes."

"How long will you be?"

This was posed more as a statement than a question. For a brief instant, because this seemed to be happening to him too much, Peter was tempted to put the phone down and once again get this unsolicited intruder out of his life. Common sense barely won the day. Eric could make life very difficult for him: he had already come to that conclusion. Why make a bad situation any worse?

"I'll be there by eleven thirty."

"Good. Tell the gate man you'll be coming to my office on the lot. He'll direct you."

Click. So that was it then. The drama would continue. It would have to be important if Eric was not only working on a Saturday, Peter thought, but also whatever it was could not wait. Peter got back to the motel on Las Palmas and got himself ready and out of the door again by ten forty.

Security at the Paramount gate was practically nonexistent. The guard yawned as he explained how to reach Eric's bungalow. Surprisingly to Peter, the lot was quite busy with carpenters, scaffolders and other workers scuttling to and fro. He wondered if they got overtime for working over the weekend. Out of curiosity, he decided to peek through a door leading to a huge stage which was also a hive of activity. Several technicians were setting up camera and lighting equipment at various angles on the floor and ladders reaching toward the ceiling were carrying equipment laden crew members.

"Can I help you?" inquired a casually dressed individual of Peter.

"Yes you can. Do you happen to know Eric Dagle's office location?

I've got an appointment with him and I think I'm lost."

"You picked the right person to ask. We're setting up a promotional shot for his movie."

A look of puzzlement crept over the man's face.

"Aren't you the wrong sex for someone with an appointment with Eric?" Peter was stunned. Was his reputation as a philanderer so notorious that people he worked with would make such a remark to a stranger? Seeing Peter's expression, the technician laughed. Taking him by the arm and leading him to a door at the other side of the stage he pointed, "Down there, second on the left and he'll be in the first bungalow you come to. His name is on the front. You can't miss it, it's a white door."

"Thanks."

Eric's bungalow/office was indeed easy to find. Twin beds of yellow geraniums carefully tended lay on each side of three steps leading up to the front porch. Peter knocked on the door and a female voice responded.

"Come in."

A young woman was pounding away on an electric typewriter on the right side of the room. Two doors fronted separate sections behind her which were partitioned. Pointing to the right hand door she said.

"Are you Peter?"

"Yes. Good morning. How are you?"

"Fine. He's expecting you. Go on through," she pointed in the direction of the right hand door.

Eric was practicing golf putts at the far side of a lavishly decorated room. An oak desk covered with scripts and other documents was next to a window overlooking the lot.

Two television sets which were both showing what appeared to be separate golf tournaments in progress occupied two corners of the room. Without looking up, Eric greeted Peter with a 'Hi' and pointed with his putter to a cushioned red leather chair on the other side of his desk. He returned to his putting and firmly struck the ball along the carpet into a paper cup from about twelve feet.

Peter attempted small talk.

"You're up early for a Saturday."

"I try to get up early every day, Peter. It doesn't always happen but I do try."

Peter could not resist the opportunity to ask the question that had been on his mind since the previous evening and he could not contain himself any longer.

"How could you be so calm and collected up at Richard's house last night after what happened earlier on at the motel?"

Eric went over to the door leading to the outer room to make sure it was firmly closed before returning to sit at his desk opposite Peter.

"I can assure you that I may have looked cool but I was anything but that inside. That's why I needed you up there to hear what had gone down after I left. Richard knew I was in town and if I'd not made an appearance, it would have caused more problems for me. He would have been extremely surprised because I never miss his pre-Golden Globes party if I'm here. What is probably even more important, I value his friendship too much to give him a fake excuse for not showing up. As far as you're concerned, it's perhaps just as well that the motel owner fired you as it's given you an excuse not to go back there again.

"I've got to pick up my weeks pay that he owes me."

"That's not a good idea. How much does he owe you?"

"About a hundred and fifty dollars."

"Okay. I'll give it to you." Eric reached for his wallet.

"Look, maybe you don't understand him like I do. I know what he's like. The same way you had to come to the party last night, I've got to go back there to get my money. He'll be very suspicious if I don't. I'm sure he'll tell the cops if I don't show. Anyway, maybe he'll change his mind and let me come back. As you know, I'm unemployed right now."

"That's the reason I want to see you Peter, I've got a job for you. I'm waiting for Tommy to get here so we can both talk to you."

Looking at his watch, Eric continued, "She should be here in about five minutes. In case you wondered, nobody, but nobody, knows what happened yesterday afternoon except us"

"Like I told you, I'm not saying anything. You don't have to worry about me."

"Good. Now tell me about David's little adventure last night."

Eric chuckled and stroked his chin as he said that and Peter wondered what part of the human psyche it was that created such pleasure in a person when hearing of other people's misfortunes. The Germans have a good word for it: 'Schadenfreude', he remembered.

Reluctantly, Peter described the incident in the garden, leaving out the most graphic details but remarking how unlucky it was for the couple for Richard to have caught them, as well as the embarrassment felt by himself in having been an involuntary witness.

He was unprepared for Eric's response.

"I would say 'poor David' except that he will benefit from this in a way."

"How come?"

"Well, first of all you've got to remember that we're in Hollywood, not some backwoods small town in the Midwest. He'll have a certain kind of notoriety for a short while. The incident will be alluded to in the trade press next week as I've already told you and then after a suitably brief interval he will come back stronger than ever. This is a very forgiving town where past transgressions are concerned and as for him personally, he's a big boy and will get over the temporary shame."

Peter wondered for a split second whether Eric was including his own episode the day before in this philosophical theory but dismissed it from his mind as quickly as it had arrived. In any event, he wasn't about to ask.

"I'm worried about Lucy. She's taken it badly and is kinda down on herself right now."

Eric didn't miss a beat as he responded, "Well, better than to be down on herself than on anyone else for awhile." He paused, looking quite pleased at his little joke, before continuing. "I don't know how she feels, but if I were her I'd lay low for a bit and hope that the whole thing blows over. It might even be a good idea for her to leave town for a couple of weeks."

Peter was appalled by this callous reaction but as Lucy had been a willing participant in the matter, there really wasn't a great deal that he could say in her defence. Hearing a loud female voice in the outer office provided a welcome opportunity, he thought, for the subject to be changed. Eric sprang up from his desk with the agility of a much younger man and pulled open the door between the two rooms.

"Tom-Tom! Do you remember our young friend?"

"I certainly do."

"Did you have a good time last night?" she asked.

"Oh yes, thanks, it was really great," Peter lied.

Eric wasted no time getting to the point once the formalities were dispensed with. Pulling another chair closer to the desk, Tommy who was dressed almost exactly the same as the previous evening, sat down and opened the black leather briefcase she was carrying and pulled out some official looking papers which she handed over to Eric.

"You know, Peter," Eric said, "you can be a great help to us. We're going to Las Vegas on Tuesday to begin shooting a film called 'BLACKJACK' on mafia influence in the gambling industry and I want you to come and work for me as my assistant on the production. How does that sound to you?"

"That sounds great but as you know I don't have any experience in the movie business. What exactly would you want me to do?"

" Just help me with the annoying little things that tend to crop up that I don't have time to deal with, like for example, travel arrangements, paying hotel bills, organizing appointments for me, that sort of thing."

"You mean you trust me that much? You don't know me very well; in fact you hardly know me at all."

"Let me tell you something, young man. It doesn't take me very long to form an opinion about someone. I've got a lot of experience in that department. Anyway," Eric leaned forward conspiratorially as if to relay a secret even though they were not alone. "I've got an idea for you to have a little walk-on part in the movie, nothing big – you understand, I may even give you a couple of lines. How'd you like that?"

In less than twenty four hours, Peter thought ironically, I've gone from working in a downmarket Hollywood motel to be an upmarket movie star.

"Don't you have to be in a union to get lines in a movie, even to be an extra?"

Eric made a gesture as if swatting a fly. "Don't worry, I'll take care of that, it's only paperwork. I'll arrange it personally." He leant toward him again as if he still didn't want Tommy to hear what he was saying which would have been rather a bizarre situation as she was only three feet away.

"I think that that would be a good way to make sure you stick around!"

More laughter as Eric continued, "Tommy has a proposition for you as well; this is the other reason I invited you up here today. Go ahead Tom-Tom, the floor is yours."

"It's not difficult, Peter," she began, "but we need you help with our co-producer Dan."

"What sort of help?"

Tommy looked over at her employer.

"Should I start at the beginning?"

"Absolutely. I'm sure Peter realizes that whatever we tell him is in strictest confidence."

He barely glanced at Peter this time as if to imply that their young visitor knew the score and that he was interested in hearing the details.

I'm learning fast, Peter thought. He was under the impression that he was going to work on a film. Could they want him to work on a human being as well?

Tommy pressed on.

"Dan Johnson is a highly successful producer who has worked with us on many movies. His devotion to a specific project is legendary. Unfortunately for us, his friends and business associates, he has developed a personal relationship with someone he met on location in Miami who describes himself as a doctor and who has developed a very negative influence on him. He's living on Dan's estate and appears to have taken control over his day to day existence. Not only is this worrying to us because he's taking our partner's mind away from what we need him to do here but he's apparently encouraging him to diminish his role in Las Vegas where his responsibilities lie in respect of our joint production."

"How do I fit in?"

Eric interceded, "I told Dan on Thursday that I'd be bringing over our confirmed shooting schedule today to go through it with him and he's expecting me at four p.m. We need you to take it over in the limo. Red will take you there and will wait for you. I'll explain on the phone that I'm in meetings and can't get away so I'm sending you as my new assistant instead. I'll go through the main points with you so you'll be able to discuss them with him extensively. Try to establish, at the very least, a cordial relationship with him. See where his mind is at and whether he has any inclination not to come over with us. Do you think you can handle that?

A light bulb suddenly switched on in Peter's mind.

"You don't want me to have sex with him do you?, because that is something that I'm not prepared to do."

Peter surprised himself with the forcefulness of his interjection.

"No, Peter not at all, but thank you for asking. By the way, I'm paying you four hundred dollars cash right now for doing this."

Peter didn't like the sound of the plan at all.

"Won't it seem strange that you're cancelling a meeting at the last minute and sending someone up to him that he's never laid eyes on before in his life?" He was very suspicious of the whole scenario and was not at all convinced that the money was not a pay off for what he was expected to do at this man's house.

"He's not in a position to find it odd. He knows that neither Tommy nor I like his friend very much and he's in the dog house with me anyway because he skipped an important meeting with us a couple days ago, claiming he was indisposed." Out of the corner of his eye Peter could see Tommy rolling her eyeballs in exasperation. He decided that this was the right time to play his trump card. Whatever the other two were up to, they obviously needed him for this little project so they were unlikely to turn down his request, in effect a miniature quid pro quo.

"Actually I need your help too. A small favor. It's for Lucy really. A frown developed on Eric's forehead

"What is it you want me to do for her?"

"I'm not so concerned about myself, but I'd like you to assure her that she will have more than a token part in the film. I don't know how these things work, I'll leave it up to you. As I mentioned, she's a little bit depressed right now and this would really cheer her up."

"You already said that."

"Yes I know, but I would be grateful if you could help."

Eric paused while he adopted what seemed to be his favorite gesture of stroking his chin.

"Maybe we could arrange something more substantial."

"Thank you."

Peter thought that at last he would be doing somebody else a good turn. But he remembered the saying that no good deed goes unpunished. Little did he know how true this would turn out to be.

CHAPTER 10

While all this had been going on, the detective in charge of the death at the motel had not been letting the grass grow under his feet. A very busy Bard indeed.

This case intrigued him for several reasons. A tough detective of the old school, David Bard had come up the hard way, joining the force as a Rover shortly after leaving school, then becoming a rookie attached to Parker Center in downtown Los Angeles. After graduation from the Police Academy, he had been sent to Boyle Heights division in West Central where he had the good fortune to come under the guidance of a savvy veteran, Jim Hendricks who taught him the ropes. After a brief stint as a patrolman, Bard became Hendricks' partner in his squad car in the gang infested section of Los Angeles known as 'the jungle', where every shift was an nerve jangling experience. Black gangs, Hispanic gangs, prostitutes, pimps, illegal aliens, slumlords, domestic partners trying to kill each other, and runaway minors proliferated. Bard saw these types of people every day.

But there were good people too, in fact the vast majority. People working hard, saving money, living peaceful lives, trying to raise families, participating in community projects. He observed them all and savored the experience. What was very important for a cop, he gradually learned, was to tell the difference between liars and truthful people, between con artists and individuals who perhaps looked at first glance to be acting suspiciously but who turned out to be just nervous or quirky by nature. After six years patrolling the area, a particularly brutal murder in his district occurred when a man threw his girlfriend out of a eighth story hotel window on fifth and Spring after an argument. This prompted Bard to decide that he wanted to become a detective. He passed the requisite exams and completing the other necessary formalities, was transferred to Hollywood Division.

As back luck would have it, his arrival coincided that very week with a highly publicized scandal at the station on Wilcox Street involving at least seven uniformed officers. They had greedily taken it upon themselves to form a robbery ring of their own. After arresting a burglary suspect, members of this group would relieve him of his ill gotten gains but would also then return to the scene of the crime and help themselves to proceeds not yet stolen or 'removed' from the premises. These were mostly shops on or near Hollywood Boulevard but sometimes also private homes where the owners had been out of town at the time of the break-ins. The 'Hollywood Seven' as these rogue officers came to be known were eventually apprehended, tried and convicted but the scandal soured the atmosphere between the public and the Division for about three years afterwards.

It was in this atmosphere that Bard arrived at his new post where he found that, to his amazement, the slightly more congenial surroundings were polluted by a massive influx of prostitutes, almost totally on Sunset Boulevard from Vine to Fairfax, a main artery of his District. The sheer quantity of women of all shapes and sizes, from as young as twelve to as well worn as sixty plus caught him by surprise and he began to wonder if he was going to be sucked in by the boring paperwork involved duties connected to this type of criminal activity.

Bard was actually grinding his molars in frustration for lack of an interesting case to sink his teeth into when the motel homicide fortuitously came into his domain that blustery Friday afternoon.

Many years ago, Hendricks had prepared him for the need to experience days, even weeks, of unending routine before a sudden jolt of action, which could possibly be life threatening, exploding literally in front of him. 'Stay awake and alert at all times' the older man counseled him, 'even if you have to drink a dozen cups of coffee on your shift. Never relax your guard for a single second, there's always going to be someone out there who's willing to hurt you.'

It was not the first time that Bard had visited this particular motel. Like others in the area, The Best Inn was Korean owned but several motels had proprietors from other countries such as India, Pakistan, Afghanistan and China. Cultural clashes

70

often caused problems such as explaining California law regarding this type of business but Bard rapidly came to the conclusion that motel owners very often pleaded ignorance to rules and regulations, conveniently citing language difficulties. In fact, they were almost always only too well aware of what was legal and what was not. The main example of this was in the controlling of prostitution on the premises. Owners were more than intelligent enough to realize that they could not rely on a steady flow of tourists to insure a regular legitimate income. The presence of the multitude of 'working girls' in the area created a constant source of revenue by virtue of their clients coming in for brief sexual assignations. A regular procedure would be for a girl to rent a room for example, at four p.m. and as check out time was usually eleven a.m. the next day, she would have ample time to service several clients during that period.

The police had two weapons to deal with this phenomenon. In the first instance, they would systematically send squad cars up and down Sunset to arrest and charge girls under the misdemeanour of 'engaging in prostitution' and courts would gradually increase the punishment in respect of and in proportion to repeat offenders. In theory, this was a plan to decrease the numbers on the street, but in practice proved to be only partly effective because the places of the women arrested and detained were invariably taken by others drawn to the area by a steady demand for their services. The second measure was to threaten owners of motels in writing with closure if evidence of considerable use of the premises for prostitution existed. In fact, some establishments in the Koreatown area of Los Angeles southeast of Hollywood had suffered this fate.

But loopholes existed in this procedure as well. It had to be proven beyond a reasonable doubt under the relevant statute that the motel owner knew that an over abundance of prostitutes were a significant proportion of the clientele on a regular basis. In the case of The Best Inn, Ky rarely made an appearance and usually sent over one of his minions to bring the weekly paychecks for the desk clerks and the maids to La Brea. As for the cash revenue, this was picked up by a courier from the bank at noon every day, including Sundays.

However, LAPD would use the most convenient way to inform a motel owner that his property was being used as a brothel to an extent that was totally unacceptable and his failure to address the problem in a timely fashion would result in closure of the site for an unspecified period. The Best Inn, along with other local motels, had been under police observation for some time although in this instance the threat of termination of business was an option that the Division had not yet applied. Ky owned two motels in Koreatown that had suffered that fate, so he was well aware of the high percentage of probability of this happening again.

What made this case different to Bard was that the dead girl didn't look like a hooker. The autopsy would attribute the cause of death as strangulation but it offered up several other points as well. Her body was in good condition, toe and fingernails manicured, teeth sound, hair well groomed, no evidence of drug taking, no needle marks on the arms or buttocks or any other tell-tale signs of unhealthy behavior.

He had got lucky early on Saturday morning when he had been able to trace the deceased's family in Wisconsin through the help of the Madison Police Department. Her mother and older sister were due to fly in later that afternoon to make a positive ID of the body. Earlier, he had made arrangements to meet their plane at LAX so that everything could be taken care of, including accommodation.

Hopefully, they would not want to stay at the motel, Bard wryly thought to himself. He didn't think it likely, but stranger things had happened. He booked a double room for two nights in a small hotel in a pleasant area in West Hollywood. The couple could extend their stay if they needed to. Nevertheless, because family members of a victim often insist on visiting the scene of the crime as soon as possible, Bard sensed that the motel would be the factor most on their minds, and so it proved.

The appearance of the two women was not quite what the detective had envisioned: to put it quite simply, Catherine Mack's mother was a statuesque beauty in her mid forties while her twenty four year old daughter was not bad looking either. Just my luck, Bard thought when he collected them at the airport. To meet two attractive women in such circumstances was indeed unfortunate. Recently divorced, he was now much more a ladies man than ever but his long hours of work made it very difficult for him to meet much eligible cock fodder outside of the force.

The detective came off the Freeway at La Brea and drove north. To relieve the sombre atmosphere in the car, he attempted some small talk.

"Is this your first time in L.A.?"

"Yes", they both replied without any emotion.

A silence resumed as Bard was careful not to chatter in case he sounded too frivolous. The mother who introduced herself as Claudia Mack at the airport gradually overcame her numbness.

"Can we go straight to where Catherine died, before we check into our hotel?"

"Yes, of course"

"Do you know why my daughter was killed, detective?"

Her curiosity gave Bard the opportunity he had hoped for and he recounted everything he knew from the moment he entered the motel the day before. As far as answering the question was concerned, he decided that he would be up front with the women in the hope that they would appreciate his honesty and give him some background on Catherine's life.

"Quite frankly, Mrs. Mack, we don't know. What we do know is that it may, just may, have been a horrible accident. What we also know is that your daughter, and forgive me for this, came to the room to meet with someone, and that that someone is responsible for her death."

The deceased girl's sister, Patricia, finally spoke.

"She told us that she was in acting school and working at a film studio. I spoke with her on Wednesday when she called me from her apartment..." she left her sentence unfinished.

Bard turned around to face the women briefly as a thought suddenly occurred to him.

"Did she live alone?"

"No, she had a roommate. I spoke to her a couple of times when Catherine was out."

"Do you have her phone number?"

"Yes, here it is."

"The younger woman handed Bard a piece of paper.

"I thought you would need it; there's an address I wrote down as well."

"Thanks; this helps a lot."

Bard parked the car around the side of the motel on Lanewood Street next to a black limousine with a young red haired man dozing in the driver's seat. The detective thought he recognized him but he couldn't place the face.

In the lobby, Peter was talking to the clerk but the conversation was not going well.

"What are you doing here. I thought you'd been fired."

"I've come to pick up my back pay, I usually get it weekly but it's not here."

"I've got a feeling you're going to have to wait a while this time, Peter" the detective interjected having overheard the conversation as he walked in. He decided to come straight to the point. Introducing the two women, he immediately put Peter on the spot.

"This was the last person to see your daughter alive, that we have spoken to, anyway. Right, Peter?"

"Yes."

"Can we see the room, please?" the girl's mother whispered. Peter looked at the clerk who looked at

Bard who nodded. Clearly shaken, the clerk cleared his throat.

"I'm sorry, that room is occupied at this time."

Bard didn't know whether to be relieved or sorry. Resisting the obvious temptation of asking whether it was a two hour special, he turned to the women.

"It's okay, we can come back tomorrow. I'll arrange it through one of my officers." He gave a meaningful look to the clerk, as if to say, there better not be a problem with that.

Turning back to Peter, his expression changed.

"I'm very glad we bumped into you. I need to speak with you. Are you still staying at your guest house?"

Peter nodded, "Yes."

"I've got an idea. I'm taking these ladies to the Tropicana on Santa Monica Boulevard. I suggest you come with us and we can speak on the way back."

"I can't. I'm being taken to see a guy about a job and it can't wait".

Bard handed Peter his card.

"Call me Monday morning at ten a.m. without fail. Don't make me have to come and look for you."

Great, thought Peter, now I may have to go into hiding. At least he won't know I'm in Las Vegas, maybe things will blow over by then.

Peter didn't really convince himself for a second though. He just knew that this wasn't going to happen.

Bard turned to the women.

"Ladies, it's getting late. I'll need you to ID Catherine's body tomorrow downtown, if that's okay. Let me take you over to your hotel and get you settled in for the night."

Once again, he turned to the clerk.

"Are you here tomorrow?"

"Yes, sir."

"Good, then we'll see you then."

He ushered the two women out into the courtyard without another word to Peter. Passing the limo, he made a mental note of the California registration license plate which he wrote into his notebook when he got into the car. One day, Bard reckoned, we'll have computers in LAPD cars that can give us all the information we need immediately.

After dropping off the women, coming down Santa Monica Boulevard on his way back to the station, Bard got a call on his car phone. One of his informants had called Wilcox to say he had something very important he wanted to discuss with him straightaway. The detective pulled into a gas station and used the pay phone to call the man, who lived on Crenshaw Boulevard. His news was what Bard had hoped for. He had previously put out feelers on his principal suspect Chester's whereabouts and now he had been spotted at a nightclub on Adams with some of his cronies less than an hour before. Bard knew the place well as a very successful black hangout.

As he sped south on Fairfax down to Wilshire, Bard called for back up. Chester may have been aware that he was 'wanted' and although he was not known to be violent, he would possibly try to resist arrest. Bard didn't want to run the risk of losing him. Turning left on Wilshire, the Saturday night traffic began to increase and Bard decided to put the siren on the roof of his Chevy. As he got near to Adams he removed the siren and drove the final two blocks to the club and turned into the parking lot. The bouncer at the door stared as the detective approached but after flashing his badge, he was waved through. Inside, it took him a couple of minutes to adjust to the lighting as a dim spotlight lit the stage on the other side of the room.

Three sultry girls dressed in short spangly silver dresses were midway through a song and dance routine accompanied by a four piece combo.

The room was small, smoky and packed with a bar on one side and large mirrors on all four walls to give the appearance of a bigger space. Tables were placed all around the front of the stage, all full with the bar area equally crowded.

Bard started to look around carefully without drawing too much attention to himself. Perhaps surprisingly, very few of the totally black customers paid him any attention, involved as they were with what was happening on stage or talking to each other. This place was a little up-market for Chester, Dan thought; what was a street pimp doing here? It didn't seem to make a lot of sense. Before he had time to chew on this, Bard spotted him. There was no mistaking the handsome face of the man who Bard had testified against a year earlier as being a minor player in a drug distribution case downtown. Chester had escaped with a suspended sentence on that occasion. He was standing at the door leading to the kitchen as Bard approached him. He decided to make his move right away before attracting attention by using his radio in the club to announce his position. Instinctively putting his right hand into the side pocket of his coat to make sure that his '38 was available just in case, he got to within three feet of his quarry.

"Chester, I need to talk to you."

Chester turned around in surprise.

"What about, man?"

"You fit the description of a person who was at The Best Inn Motel on La Brea yesterday afternoon. Also, to think of it, he had your name as well."

"Is that right?"

Bard didn't answer the question. There wasn't any need to. "Can we go outside? It's very noisy in here."

"Why not?" Gesturing with his left hand, "After you."

Bard declined the offer, instead asking "Where is the nearest exit?"

"Over there," Chester pointed to a side entrance of the club. As Bard turned to retrace his steps, Chester shoved him hard with his right hand in between his shoulder blades. The detective crashed forward into a table where three people were having dinner. Chester darted behind the bandstand and threw himself through a door leading to the outside of the club.

Bard cursed. He picked himself up and gave chase running right through the stage where the singers were winding down their performance and out the same exit that Chester had used to escape. He sprinted through the door knocking over a waiter carrying some plates of food and rushed out.

It was pitch black outside, but Bard ran in the direction of barking dogs down the street. A squad car, its tires squealing, hurtled around the corner.

The detective waved it down and jumped in the back..

"Male, black, five foot nine, in late twenties or early thirties, well dressed. Put out an APB," he spat out. "Do we have a chopper available?"

"Coming up right now, sir. We asked for assistance less than ten minutes ago," the officer replied. Almost as soon as his sentence was finished, the police helicopter was sending down its broad beam of light over the club area and beyond. But it was too late. After a half hour search of the area, the exercise was suspended. The bird had flown. For now.

CHAPTER 11

Winding up Sunset Boulevard into Beverly Hills for the second time in 24 hours, Peter realized that his life had spun completely out of control. Nothing made sense anymore. Now he was being asked, or more realistically being told, with the temptation of another bribe, to probe into someone's life style for no other reason than it fitted into his benefactor's plans. Eric had given him an hour's briefing on the script details and provided him with notes that he could refer to during his meeting with Dan. He also insisted that he must extract a promise from him that he would be ready to travel to Las Vegas with the film crew on Tuesday afternoon.

The road on Sunset led to a right turn up to Bel Air which featured houses even more luxurious than the ones he had swept by on the way to the previous night's party. On Stone Canyon Road, Red took the limo up a steep ascent onto a private driveway of exclusive mansions.

It's always worth seeing where a millionaire resides, thought Peter; now I know what it looks like to be part of this rarefied world. A winding road led to the right till the houses became few and far between. Just before the very top which terminated in a cul-de-sac, were granite stone walls on the left hand side of the street in the middle of which were a pair of black iron gates. Red drove up to the entrance and got out of the limo to press a button on a bronze plaque located on one side of the wall. After a pause, a voice crackled in response.

"Johnson residence."

"Hi, I'm here with some documents from Eric Dagle for Mr.Johnson."

"Just a moment."

After considerably more than a moment, in fact more like two minutes, the voice returned.

"Drive to the top of the hill. When you see the garage, turn right and park next to the jeep."

"Thank you."

Red returned to the limo while the gates were opening inward electronically. Peter presumed that the house they were visiting would be visible from the entrance, but he was wrong. It took almost a minute to get to the brow of the hill before the mansion came into view. Twin turrets situated on either side of a three storey faux nineteenth century castle reminded him of an old English black and white film he had once seen in Columbus many years ago. This palatial abode could well have been built in an attempt to reproduce that bygone European era. Red parked as per his instructions.

"You go in, Peter; I'm still tired after last night and I need to catch up on my sleep. If you have any problems you know where to find me."

"I hope I do know where to find you. This looks like a pretty big spread." Wouldn't it be convenient, Peter thought, not for the first time, if someone marketed sophisticated pocket size phones that people could talk to each other on from a distance. It would save a lot of trouble. He approached what he presumed was the front door but it was such a big house that he couldn't be sure. Instead of a bell, there was a huge bronze door knocker in the shape of a lion head.. He knocked once. Gently. After a brief interval the door opened and Peter found himself face to face with a pleasant looking individual in his 30's with long brown hair and a tanned face who was dressed in white shorts and white cotton short sleeved shirt. He looked like he were about to play a game of tennis.

"Are you Peter, by any chance?"

"Yes I am. Good afternoon."

"Dan's expecting you; he's out by the pool. I'll show you the way."

"Thank you."

Peter wondered if it was going to be a long journey, judging by the size of the house.

"He's taking a nap as he is still recovering from last night. We had some people around and it took us forever to get rid of them. Buy the way, I'm Dominic. I live in the cottage you probably spotted on the way up the drive."

"Have you known Dan a long time?"

"About a year and a half. I'm a doctor. I met Dan professionally and we seemed to hit it off so he very kindly offered me some accommodation after I split with my ex. This way I can keep an eye on him." Dominic laughed as if that were a very funny remark. I bet you can, thought Peter. His companion led Peter through the living room which was in a state of disarray with cushions and chairs everywhere. A large number of half empty liquor bottles and glasses were scattered around on tables all around the room. As they passed the kitchen area, Peter glimpsed at a huge collection of dirty plates and cutlery piled up in two sinks. It must have been quite a bash, he thought. Dominic caught Peter's glance into the kitchen.

"Afraid the place is in a hell of a mess," he interjected with a shrug of his shoulders. "We kept the hired help up very late so I gave them the day off today." He grinned sheepishly. Peter noticed that the man used the first person singular. Does that mean that he's in charge of everything else, he wondered.

The pool area was deserted. Excusing himself, Dominic went back into the house after assuring his guest that Dan would be there in a minute. Peter could hear his voice reverberating from some distance away.

"Eric's friend is here. He's waiting for you by the pool"

This sounded more like an admonition than a request for an appearance. After a minute or two, Dan emerged through the French windows leading on to the terrace. He was wearing a pale blue towelling dressing gown tied at the waist and to his visitor he bore more than a passing resemblance to Burt Reynolds. The only distinctive difference was that he had considerably more real hair on his head than that actor. He was a very heavy set individual and although he appeared to be in his mid to late fifties, looked to be in excellent physical condition except for the puffy face now creased into a smile. He advanced towards Peter.

"Ah, the Boy Wonder! Eric speaks very highly of you. What have you done to deserve this, he's usually very negative about people he meets for the first time."

"Probably because I follow his instructions precisely," responded Peter. "Like coming up here to see you at very short notice."

Dan chuckled. "Sit down, sit down, make yourself at home. I can save you a lot of time by telling you right now that the script isn't sexy enough."

"Could you be more specific?" replied Peter, taking out his notebook.

Before Dan had a chance to reply, Dominic proved Peter's earlier supposition to be correct by coming out of the house with a tennis racket and a carton of balls.

"Excuse me interrupting, but I'm going next door to get a couple of sets in with our neighbor."

Turning to Peter, he remarked "Nice to have met you."

Looking back at Dan, he wagged a finger in his direction. "Don't forget we have a dinner appointment and she doesn't like to be kept waiting." Kissing Dan lightly on the cheek, he waved at Peter briefly and disappeared back into the house.

"What was it you were asking me; oh yes, about the script. Look, young man, we're making a film in Las Vegas about people who live there. It isn't called Sin City for nothing. We need more T and A than we've got right now. Perhaps, a small role for an actress who could portray a foxy young lady of easy, very easy, virtue."

Peter had an inspiration.

"If you're serious, I know just the person for this part. She's really very pretty and I'm sure she could learn lines quickly. Isn't it a bit late in the day, though, to introduce a new character?"

"You've asked me two questions in one sentence; the answer in correct order is 'yes' and 'no'. Does that make sense?"

"Um…I think so."

"Good. Let's celebrate."

Dan got up from his pool chair and went into the living room momentarily before coming back with a small silver bowl full of cocaine and a miniature mahogany box which he placed on the table between them.

"Care for a toot?"

Peter was caught unawares by this question and although he had no experience of the drug, it would have appeared to be extremely ungracious to turn the offer down. Sensing his uncertainty, Dan smiled.

"Don't worry, it may not be legal, but it's not going to kill you."

Taking out a hundred dollar bill from the pocket of his robe, he gestured towards Peter.

"I always like to use a C- note. The bigger the bill, the higher the high."

He proceeded to chop out four lines on the glass table between them with a razor blade that he had produced from the box.

He then put the note to his left nostril and inhaled enthusiastically, repeating the procedure with his right. He passed the note to Peter with a satisfied grin.

Peter followed his host's manoeuvre. He decided to ingest as little as possible, but even so, the numbing jolt of the powder seared his septum with a sensation he had never felt before in his life.

"Quick, quick, do the other side now."

Dan's exhortation fulfilled, Peter immediately felt that his nose was no longer part of his face. The feeling only lasted for a minute as the particles travelled up towards his brain. He began to feel light-headed, and dare he admit to himself a very pleasant glow enveloping him.

"How does that feel?"

"You know, it's not so bad. I feel tingly and quite comfortable."

"Good. Welcome to the world of the extreme experience. The creator of the great detective Sherlock Holmes, that wonderful writer and philosopher Sir Arthur Conan Doyle, was a great proponent of the power of chemical substances. So if it was good enough for the old boy, it sure as hell is good enough for me, not that I need him for an excuse."

After a few minutes had gone by, Peter began to come down and he suddenly realized that he had not fulfilled the task which he had been sent to Dan's house to perform. Before he had a chance to consult his files which he now put on his lap, Dan interjected.

"I'm a little confused as to why you're here instead of the grand master. He did explain to me on the phone that he was dealing with some important decisions over at Paramount. How long have you known Eric anyway, and what do you really do for him?"

Peter related the story that he and Eric had agreed on, namely that he was now his personal assistant and he would be helping as much as possible to ensure a smooth operation in Las Vegas. Dan seemed satisfied with this response and for the next hour they went through the filming schedule from Wednesday onwards. Peter extracted a promise from his host that he would be on a plane to Vegas with the ticket that he now gave him.

"Does your girlfriend have an agent?"

"I'm not sure, I don't think so."

"Not a problem. I'll call my manager tomorrow even though it's a Sunday, and get him to set something up. Have her ring me in the afternoon and I'll tell her what time to go and see him on Monday to prepare the necessary documents."

"Don't you want to meet her first; After all you're only taking my word that she is good enough for this"

"That's OK" said Dan laughing "We'll soon find out if she's not. I've got a feeling we can trust your judgement. Don't worry about her part; I'll get the writer to put in some lines for her. We've got enough time. I remember a movie called The Wild Bunch directed by Sam Peckinpah and I was once told by his assistant that the old boy was constantly creating new dialogue while he was in the middle of filming in the desert."

Dan got up indicating that the meeting was over.

"I'm very grateful to you for this and I'm sure she will be even more so."

"It's a pleasure. I'll see you to the front door." Dan led the way back into the living room. Halfway through he grabbed Peter by his left arm.

"Look, young man, you seem to be a nice person so I'm going to be frank with you. Never mind what you said before. I need you to tell me the real reason why Eric would send you up here to discuss such an important project considering I've never met you before. Don't you think that's a bit strange?"

"What do you mean?"

"Well, I think he's trying to check up on me and have you report back to him. I know he doesn't approve of my life style, but there's not a lot he can do about it. It's my production company and it's my money funding this film. Whatever Eric has told you about our business relationship, I'm the one calling the shots."

"He didn't say anything about that at all." Peter prevaricated, but as soon as the words were out of his mouth, he regretted them. Too late now.

Dan continued. "Well, that's as may be, but I don't care what he thinks, and I don't have any problem if you pass on what I have said to you. I like the guy a lot, but he's always been capable of behaving in a bizarre way if it suits him." Patting Peter gently on the back while opening the front door, he concluded, "I advise you to watch your step. See you on Tuesday."

With that remark, Dan closed the door and went back into the house. It wasn't until Red was driving him back down the hill that Peter realized that his new acquaintance was the first person with whom he had come into contact in the last 36 hours of his crazy new life, apart from Lucy, who had not asked him to do a favor for them.

CHAPTER 12

Peter got back to his hotel room at about midnight and was so exhausted that he collapsed on his bed and fell asleep immediately with his clothes on. The next thing he knew according to the clock radio by the bed that it was 10 a.m. Sunday morning. Looking out of his window at a gray sky threatening to pour down with rain, he realized with a jolt that he was still carrying a large amount of cash on him. There was nothing he could do about it until his bank on Sunset and Vine opened on Monday morning. On coming downstairs, he found a message from Bard, requesting him to call right away. Peter was glad he did not have a phone in his room and he decided to wait till later in the day to return the call. He was not surprised by this development, as he knew the detective would be wanting to speak to him again very soon.

Peter set off, after grabbing a quick breakfast, to Lucy's apartment to tell her about Dan's offer. Fortunately for him, he had made a note of the address when leaving the house the previous morning. On arrival, he rang her doorbell. No answer. He tried again with a longer ring. Still no luck. She may have gone out, even for the day, so he decided to leave a note in her letterbox. Great news! he wrote. The executive producer on Eric's film says he can give you more than a walk-on with the possibility of a few lines. The film crew is leaving for Vegas on Tuesday and you could be with them. Call Devin Malone at 310 550-2661 early tomorrow to set up an appointment for Monday. If you wish further details contact me by tonight. Best wishes,

Peter. He included his phone number at the motel in the message.

That should do it, he thought. If she doesn't respond to such good news, she would have to be a zombie. Mission sort of accomplished, he had a brainwave. Yes, another one. The guilt level connected to his part in the conspiracy to conceal the true nature of the events at The Best Inn was gradually rising. He decided to contact Catherine's mother and sister in order to reassure them that he would do whatever he could to find the person responsible for her death. He couldn't do that right away, obviously, but at least he could go through the motions and perhaps that would help him get off the hook as well.

Wishful thinking, of course, but you never know, Peter reflected. He remembered that Bard was going to take the couple downtown in the morning to the morgue for purpose of identification. As they would not exactly be in a mood for sightseeing, with a bit of luck they would be back at the hotel soon, the name of which the detective had inadvertently disclosed the previous afternoon. This time, Peter got lucky. It was shortly after lunch time when he got there and he correctly guessed they would not be going too far to get something to eat. He found them sitting at the back of the coffee shop, Dukes, which was on the ground floor of the hotel situated up a gentle slope north of Santa Monica Boulevard in what was obliquely known as the 'gay' part of town. Approaching the couple tentatively, he was not at all sure what reaction he would get. As he reached the table the women looked up.

"Hi, I don't know if you remember me. I met you both at the La Brea motel yesterday afternoon." He had previously decided that 'how are you' or 'how're you doing' would definitely be inappropriate. It would be perfectly obvious to anyone with a grain of intelligence that they would not be doing very well and would probably not be in the mood to make any response whatsoever. Bracing himself for rejection, Peter was pleasantly surprised when Patricia looked up and with a faint smile and remarked "Hello. I remember you quite well. How'd you know where to find us? Did the detective tell you?"

Catherine's mother for her part ignored the intrusion and carried on nibbling on a salad. Answering both questions at once Peter replied

"Well, I overheard him say where he was taking you. I wasn't sure if you would appreciate my coming here but I decided to take the chance just in case. The worst that could happen is that you could tell me to get lost. I very much wanted to give you some information which might be of use to you."

"What exactly do you mean?"

"Apart from being very concerned that I was the clerk who sent your sister up to the room ..."

He broke off unable to complete the sentence. The younger woman stared at him without saying anything. He regained his composure and decided to run the risk of implicating himself.

"That guy the police are looking for - I don't think he was responsible for your sister's death."

"What makes you say that? The detective said they have very good case against him."

"Well, I'm not so sure about that." elaborated Peter warming to the task, "First of all, he was barred permanently from the motel by the owner. I think that the only reason he was there at all was because he must have sneaked in the back way to visit a woman that he knew was staying in the motel at the time"

"How do you know that?"

"Because when I had checked that person in earlier I remembered from a previous occasion that they knew each other. He wasn't supposed to be anywhere near the motel but I was on my own at the desk and I don't see everything that goes on."

"So who do you think killed my sister? After all, the detective told us that you gave that guy's description to him? Why are you saying something different now?"

Her mother, by now, was staring at him also waiting for his answer.

"Well, I noticed when I came on my shift at work, that someone had booked the room that your sister occupied earlier in the day but never checked in."

After a brief pause to let this sink in, Peter continued.

"According to the maid she thought she saw a man in the vicinity of your sister's room before I came on duty although I never saw him myself."

"Did you tell the detective about this?"

"I don't believe I mentioned it, no."

Catherine's mother spoke for the first time.

"Why not? Didn't you think it was important?"

"To tell you the truth," Peter continued defensively, "I didn't remember it at the time, but I did last night and I now realise it could be very significant ."

"We spoke to Catherine's roommate today," the mother interjected, "she really wasn't very helpful. Someone may have told her not to say anything after she reported my sister missing on Saturday morning. However, she told us that Catherine always called her if she was going to be out all night and when she saw on the television what happened she contacted the police to find out if it could be her."

The older woman started to weep gently and Peter suddenly realized that he rather be anywhere else in the world at that moment. Oh God, he thought, I'm really in a mess now. Taking as his mental cue that 'necessity is the mother of invention' he decided to gamble even further. After all, he had to do something to relieve some of the guilt that had been enveloping him.

"Look, I have an idea. The detective left a message at my place that he wanted to speak to me urgently. I'm going to call him this afternoon and tell him everything that I left out before. I know it's not going to be a great comfort to you, but maybe, just maybe, we can find out the truth. Hopefully, it will give you a small amount of satisfaction if," Peter looked at the women hopefully as he spoke, "we can bring the right person to justice who was responsible for your daughter's death."

The mother stared hard at Peter.

"According to what we managed to get out of the roommate, Catherine had a different life to the one she discussed with us on the phone. She said she was a secretary at Paramount Studios but she couldn't take phone calls from us there as she would get into trouble, so we never called her at work. However, according to the roommate, Irene, they were both doing escort work. She refused to explain exactly what that involved but the detective has told us that this type of work can be very dangerous," She hesitated before continuing, "and often involves having to have sex with clients."

"Really?" Peter uttered the single word as if this was a great revelation to him but this news was not exactly unexpected. When Catherine had come into the motel on Friday, she wasn't hesitant or nervous in any way. On the contrary, despite her youthful appearance and her not displaying some of the more hardened characteristics of a prostitute, she seemed to be very composed.

"That's why," her mother continued, "your story makes some sense to me as Catherine would be very unlikely to be involved with any street person which is what this suspect appears to be."

"How long do you expect to be in town?" asked Peter anxious to get the focus away from himself.

"Well, my mother wants to go home tomorrow but I'm going to stay for the inquest so I guess the answer to that question would be, for a few more days," explained Patricia.

"I'm going to be in town till Tuesday afternoon so would it be okay if I called you tomorrow to pass on any developments from my end?"

"Sure. I'll probably be hearing from the detective tonight but you can call if you want."

With that semi-encouraging response, Peter felt it was appropriate to leave with a final expression of regret which he tried to make sound sincere. Looking at both women he made an effort.

"I can't tell you how sorry I am about all this, I'll do anything I can to help." The couple watched silently as he exited the cafe. He decided against going back to check on Lucy. It was up to her now, he'd done his bit to help her and she now had to help herself.

On the spur of the moment, Peter decided to call Red. He wanted to show his appreciation for ferrying him around for the last couple of days by inviting him for a late lunch. Red suggested that they meet at Schwab's Drugstore on the corner of Sunset and Crescent.

Sitting down at a table at the world famous location, he tried to fill Peter in on its history.

"A lot of professionals in the film business swing by here regularly including some famous names. Saturday between 10 and 5 is the time this place is really hopping and sometimes you have to wait up to an hour for a table. You see those telephone booths back there?" continued Red, gesturing to the back wall on the left of the counter. "Some people use them as their office and can talk for ages. Over there at the counter is supposed to be where Lana Turner was discovered by an agent at the age of sixteen. It's bullshit." Red snorted derisively. "She went to Hollywood High School further down Sunset and used to hang out at a Mom and Pop coffee shop next to next to the school where a photographer who was a regular took some shots of her one day and had them published in a local paper. The rest, as they say, is history."

Peter remained silent while he ate, soaking up the atmosphere and checking out the cast of characters floating in and out of his line of vision. He noticed that a lot of people were just sitting around talking and not being bothered by the waitresses who flitted about periodically greeting some customers by name and refilling their cups without being asked to.

"Is this Golden Globes awards deal tonight worth going to?" Peter asked.

"Well, yes and no," Red replied which didn't sound like much of an answer.

"What do you mean by that?"

"It's not on TV so if you want to see it you have to go to the show in Beverly Hills. What it is, is a bunch of reporters from other countries, I believe mostly European, telling some American film and TV actors and actresses that they think they're worthy of some kind of award for their work. These foreigners kinda lost credibility a few weeks ago when the husband of an actress nobody ever heard of took them on an all expenses paid junket to the casino he owns in Las Vegas for three days. Then they repaid his kindness by awarding his wife the title of the most promising newcomer of last year."

"No kidding!"

"Oh yeah, it actually happened. It's the only award that's announced before the show. Some people thought it was very funny, some people thought it was ridiculous and others couldn't care less."

"What's your opinion on the evening?"

"My opinion? Well, all I know is that every time they have the awards you can't find a taxi in this damn town for twentyfour hours" replied Red, laughing. "I read somewhere that some members of the organization would cross the Alps for a hot dog! And here's the funniest part; I'm willing to bet good money that one day, perhaps in as little as ten years from now, it will become as significant an event as the Oscars."

"How is that possible? From what you say it seems that not many people take it that seriously."

"Well, somebody once said that there's no such thing as bad publicity. That person was probably a Hollywood agent. Anyway, this town thrives on acclaim, even from foreigners and actors love to be told that they are good at what they do. It goes with the territory."

"Are you going?"

"Not me personally, but I'm dropping off Eric and Tommy in the limo. He did mention that you can go along with them, so why don't you? After all, I know you can't wait to see them again."

Peter looked at his companion to check if he was being sarcastic.

Maybe he was. What the hell, I might as well go, he thought. I could make some useful contacts.

CHAPTER 13

Peter had asked Red not to come to his residence to pick him up that evening as he was attracting too much attention with the flurry of phone calls he had been receiving the last couple of days. From the moment he stepped into the limo outside the Hollywood Roosevelt Hotel he could sense that Tommy was in a bad mood. While Eric appeared to support Dan's proposal regarding Lucy's participation in the movie and showed relief regarding his partner's apparent approval of the shooting schedule, Tommy had a different agenda on the boil. She continued on the way to the hotel to expand on her theme of finding a way to remove Dominic from being a 'pervasive' influence on

Dan's private life. Why is she so concerned, Peter wondered to himself. What business is it of hers anyway? Somehow he felt he was going to be involved, whether he wanted to be or not.

Inside the Beverly Hilton ballroom, celebrity guests sat and politely nibbled at their dinner which to say the least, was not very inspiring. Red had earlier derisively dismissed the occasion as another stop on the 'rubber chicken' circuit and his assessment appeared to be not too far off the mark. Peter, however, found himself amused at the phenomenon, for want of a better word, of air kissing between actresses and sometimes between men and women upon meeting each other which even to his unpractised eyes definitely appeared not to be accompanied by any emotion.

After dinner was concluded, a tall, thin, almost bald man in his sixties approached the podium on the stage to muted applause. Explaining that he was from Turkey and apologizing with a warm smile for his inability to express himself in fluent English, he droned on nonetheless for several minutes with the usual platitudes describing the importance of the occasion. Peter was only stopped from dozing off by the arrival on the stage of the comedian and star of the successful television sitcom Mork and Mindy who began his routine by yelling "Are we all still awake!" From then on, he paid a degree of attention to the hour long presentation of awards until mercifully, the proceedings eventually ground to a halt. I know what I've just witnessed, he concluded to himself, mutual masturbation in its highest art form. If all award ceremonies are like this, I'll make this my first and last appearance at one of them, grudgingly admitting to himself that he'd probably make an exception for the Academy Awards..

When he got home, he found a message from Lucy waiting for him. She would definitely make it to the meeting at the agent's office the next day and thanked him for his help. Peter was sorry to have missed her call but intended to make up for that on Monday. Not surprisingly the manager's brother who worked the night shift was very curious about Peter's new found popularity. A short older man with a trim white moustache and rimless reading glasses, he gave Peter the impression by his somewhat agitated state that he had waited up late especially to quiz him about the increased interest surrounding him. For the first two weeks of his stay, he had lived like a hermit going out to work and coming in at night to watch television in his room. The only interaction he had achieved with the old man, apart from paying his rent, was to ask for an extra blanket to get him through the chilly nights that are regularly experienced for the months of November through February in the City of Angels. Some Angels, thought Peter, they seem to have faded into obscurity as far as he was concerned. This mythical presence had yet to reverberate in his direction and most probably never would, he thought pessimistically.

He had judged the mood correctly. Steve didn't waste any time getting straight to the point. This was unfortunately not the best time to receive a managerial grilling as on the way back Red had confided in him a very interesting and possibly a very disturbing development. Red had overheard

Tommy earlier in the evening questioning Eric's judgment in placing so much trust in someone whom he hardly knew.

After all, he was just a motel clerk whom he had met by chance, she insisted, albeit a good looking one. What was so special about Peter that you wanted to make him part of the team at such short notice, she had asked. According to Red, Tommy was very sceptical about the matter and continued to voice her concerns until they arrived to pick Peter up in Hollywood. If only she knew, Peter thought, presuming, of course, that she didn't. Therefore he was not exactly in the most receptive frame of mind as he approached the desk to pick up his key, for the interrogation that followed.

"Hey man, what's going on?"

"What do you mean, Steve?"

"Well, you've been getting a lot of phone calls for the last few days, people asking for you, about you, when are you expected back, all this sort of thing. Then this afternoon my nephew got a call from a police detective who wants you to get in touch with him as soon as possible. He was asking questions about you like where you're from, how long you've been staying here, are you a good tenant, etc., etc., etc. So" Steve took a deep breath, "Can you explain all of this?"

"Yes, I can." Peter related the events of the previous Friday, except of course the most obviously incriminating factor.

"It's because a prostitute was murdered at the motel I work at, or did work at, on La Brea." Let the guy know the bare facts only, Peter thought, maybe he'll be satisfied. After all, he would have found out sooner or later, either by local newspaper reports or someone's clueing him in. At the end of his explanation of sorts, his interrogator didn't look any more convinced, but at least he stopped asking questions for the time being. Peter got the message. More than ever he needed to bail out as soon as possible. The trip to Vegas, a place he had never seen and only knew by reputation was a godsend and would provide a temporary escape from the corner of the room that he was sure that he was painting himself steadily towards.

Next morning he was up and out so early that he got to his bank on Sunset before it opened. Now he had approximately 24 hours to avoid Bard before his departure. For a moment he hoped that he was not still a top priority target for more questioning but as soon as that thought came into his head, he knew that he was being extremely unrealistic. There were really only two chances that the detective would not continue to be on his tail: slim and none, and Slim had already left town. Now that Steve knew some of the details of his situation, he had to devise a plan to leave the property without raising suspicion. Once again Peter decided to rely on the basics. He would that evening inform the night manager that because he had to find another job immediately to keep himself solvent, he was considering taking a temporary position slightly out of town. This included accommodation as well and it was too good an opportunity to pass up.

If he was pressed for more details he would go through the motions of saying how much he hoped that his room or another one would be available for him on his return and he had felt that he had been treated fairly while he had been a resident. The usual nonsense. Whether the guy would fall for this was something beyond his control but at least it would explain his sudden departure, He would also infer that he would be checking in by phone every few days for messages.

Meanwhile, across town, Lucy was entering the office building in Beverly Hills of the agent with whom she had made the appointment. Devin Malone was a man of meticulous habits. While it was true that he had not risen to his substantial position in the film industry at the 'tender' age of 30 by the often quoted and equally often used path of beginning his working life by way of the William Morris Agency mailroom, his route to the top had so far been more colorful. Shortly after leaving college at the age of 22, he had secured a position through a friend of his father's at a top agency on Beverly Boulevard near the world famous Chasen's Restaurant. To call this a position was a bit of an exaggeration, to say the least, as he very quickly found himself not a million miles away from being an indentured servant.

He was expected to arrive every day at 8.30 a.m. sharp and occasionally, even earlier, if there had been a meeting late the night before and the office needed to be tidied up. Also, if a presentation to a client was planned for that day and extra equipment had to be set up such as a cinema screen and chairs, and tables etc. it was his job to place them in a neat formation inside the conference room. He accepted this as par for the course but he was less than overjoyed at being summoned by his boss once in a while to work on a Saturday when the pressure of work necessitated an extra day at the office.

Altogether the mundane chores of the designated office junior such as sorting mail, making lunch and dinner reservations and the most ticklish of all tasks, fending off callers with whom his boss did not want to talk and had no intention of talking with, made the day a long one indeed. There were however the occasional perks. Although he was the lowest on the totem pole, he did get offered, once in a while, and did eagerly accept, film premiere tickets which invariable were followed by lavish parties. His employer, a 57 year old transplanted New Yorker who was one of the senior partners in the agency, was a workaholic who tended to regard these functions as a pain in the rear, unless, of course, they involved one of the more prestigious of his clients. One afternoon, after Devin had been working at the agency for over a year and was beginning to despair of any promotion in the foreseeable future, Mr. Big Shot summoned him into his office.

"Look, I need you to do me a favor. I promised my wife that I would take her over to a screening" he always used the word 'screening', not premiere "in Westwood tonight. I'm very tied up on a major deal involving a director back East who's just joined the agency and I urgently need to speak to him tonight when he comes off the set. My wife thinks she's in love with the star of this movie," he raised his eyebrows in a mock gesture because as Devin himself knew, the gentlemen in question was widely presumed in the industry to be a homosexual, "and she wants to go to this premiere badly. I took the liberty of telling her a few minutes ago that my assistant would be happy to be her escort. Is that going to be a problem for you?"

Yes, thought Devin, this would be a major problem for him because he had already arranged a date with the very cute secretary who fielded the front lobby of the office next door and who had only been working there for a month. This is going to look great, he thought sarcastically. I finally pluck up the courage to invite her for supper after talking to her in the elevator a few times in the last couple of weeks and now I'm standing her up on our first date. However, trying to duck out of Mr. Big Shot's demand was not an option. Devin wished that there existed a system of electronic mail that he could use to acquaint the object of his affection with this development but absent this technological device he would be forced to confront her face to face. Fortunately, she appeared to take it well and his excuse was aided by his ability to flourish the premiere tickets by way of explanation. He knew very well, however, that it would be a very good idea to make his next approach occur over a weekend when it would be more than unlikely that his 'conquest' would be interrupted by work issues. Always presuming that she had not lost interest in the meantime.

The evening did not go well. Mrs. Big Shot, unknown to Devin, was extremely suspicious about her husband's last minute defection and almost as soon as he pulled into the driveway of the couple's Coldwater Canyon home, she made her feelings abundantly clear. She was not amused and her body language immediately made it perfectly plain that she did not appreciate her having a minion as her escort for the evening. His boss's wife was at least 25 years younger than her spouse and was keen to make that point on this occasion by being fashionably dressed in a stunning black number accessorised with a gold necklace and a diamond encrusted watch.

Devin put her age in the early thirties and with her long raven hair cascading around her neck and flowing onto her shoulders, she could easily be mistaken for being a prominent actress going to her own premiere.

On the way to the theater, he did his best to make polite small talk, but was curtly rebuffed by monosyllabic responses. The irony of the situation was that her husband was indeed working late but there was no way his employee could prove it as the switchboard had closed down so that telephone contact was impossible. Devin decided that mentioning that she could page her husband would be an extremely inappropriate suggestion for him to make, so he remained silent on the topic.

The film, a long parable of life amongst some American soldiers in Vietnam produced and directed by a distinguished 'ladies man' mercifully captured her attention but Devin was so bored that he nodded off on more than one occasion. At the post screening party, his companion flirted outrageously with the leading actor while completely ignoring her escort who fortunately was able to satisfy his hunger by treating himself to a substantial helping of the catered buffet. He did however limit himself to two drinks as per his employer's instructions earlier. The same could not be said of his wife who availed herself liberally of the liquid refreshments, so much so that Devin had to help her into his car when they were leaving. If he thought her mood would lighten on the return journey, he was very much mistaken. After her being condescending in her brief moments of dialogue which included being critical of his driving skills, it was with great relief that Devin terminated his ordeal in the driveway of her home. He wasted no time coming round to the passenger door, opening it and offering his hand to help her out. Only then did a small crumb of courtesy emanate from her mouth.

"Thank you. Good night."

It wasn't much, but it was slightly better than the icy silence he had been forced to endure previously and he almost hoped that he would get such a bad report card that Mr. Big Shot would never again prevail upon him for a subsequent experience of that nature.

Next morning, he expected at the very least a query on how the evening had transpired but apart from the normal fetch and carry routine, there was silence. After a cheery 'good night' shortly after 6 p.m. Devin realized that his boss had no wish to discuss the matter. A couple of days later, while discussing the evening with a fellow employee in whom he felt he could confide, he found out that she was spouse number three and as he eventually realized, constituted a 'trophy' wife. It was also revealed to him that other employees were regularly subjected to frequent phone calls to the agency to check on her husband's whereabouts. The 'wrong' answer would often be responded to by sarcasm or varying degrees of annoyance delivered in a withering tone if her husband was not available to take her call.

Conducting a diplomatic conversation with her, however brief, in these circumstances was very stressful to Devin when he was occasionally the recipient of these calls. It seemed that the only reason that he was not inflicted with a barrage of the intensity experienced by his colleagues was that as the most junior employee he mercifully did not have a telephone extension of his own.

About five weeks after the less than gratifying premiere experience, he was summoned into his employer's office one afternoon at about 3 p.m. Handing Devin a small felt-covered jewellery box, 'Mr Big Shot' appeared to be flustered.

"This can't wait. My wife broke the clasp on her favorite bracelet and the jeweller has sent it round to me with it repaired and in mint condition. He was supposed to bring it back tomorrow but she called and asked him to drop it off at the office today. We're going to an important event at the Beverly Hills Hotel tonight and she insists on wearing it. There's a possibility that I won't be able to get away from here till 7:30 but as we were going there with neighbors, she'll be able to get there and I can meet her there later. I need you to go up to my home right now and leave it for her with the maid if she's not home. You can take the rest of the afternoon off - just go now. O.K.? Don't lose it! It's extremely expensive."

Devin did not exactly relish renewing contact with someone who had shown him so much discourtesy at their last meeting. However, this chore would only occupy an hour of his time and he would be getting home two hours early. A pity he hadn't known before as he would have swung by his new girlfriend Laurie's office next door and invited her out on a date. Approaching her at the last minute felt a bit contrived and as he was getting to know her better, little by little, he didn't want to rock the boat. He was seeing her on Friday night anyway.

Driving up Coldwater at 3:30 p.m. was no problem. The rush hour over to the San Fernando Valley had not started and a few minutes later he was cruising on Lindacrest toward the house. Turning into the driveway, he noticed the dented rear end of a gray Mustang parked almost out of sight on the right side of the spacious garage. It seemed to be an unusual choice of transportation for a house employee of the couple, Devin mused; perhaps it belonged to someone who had come to do some work on the home. He was about to ring the bell at the front door when he noticed it had been left slightly ajar. In his limited experience of the area, he had found this to be nothing out of the ordinary as it was well patrolled by armed security day and night. In any event, incidents of daytime intruders into homes in isolated patches of Beverly Hills were practically unheard of. As he entered the hallway, Devin was struck by a whimpering sound, coming from a room to his left. There was no sign of the maid or a workman but the murmur intrigued him. Perhaps it was a hungry pet that was waiting anxiously to be fed and had decided to make its feelings known.

This decision not to announce his presence immediately was something that Devin would continue to reflect on periodically for the rest of his life. For whatever reason, he retreated back out the front door and made a right turn onto the lawn from which there was a pathway to the back of the house. As he was on his way to see if there was anyone available at the rear, he momentarily glanced through a gap in the blinds covering the window of a ground floor room. It was from there that he thought he had heard the muted sounds coming. What he observed astonished, fascinated, aroused and repelled him all at the same time. To his amazement, he saw his employer's wife lying on a divan half-naked on her back with her left foot touching the floor. Her other leg was up in the air being grasped at the ankle by a naked swarthy man with a muscular build in his 30's with long black hair flowing down over his shoulders who was standing at the base of the bed. His vigorous thrusting into the woman's body increased in tempo as Devin watched mesmerized. Her whimpering grew louder and louder as she moved to climax and reached such a volume that it would have been impossible for anyone else in the house not to have become aware of the situation. Even outside a closed window, her cries of ecstasy were clearly audible. For a moment, he wondered if any of the neighbors were at home, and if so, whether they would have heard anything.

Certain that he had not been seen, Devin returned to the front of the house and re-entered the hallway. He was at a complete loss as to how to proceed, but there was one thing that he did know; he would have to make a decision in seconds, not minutes. He had to leave the bracelet behind, otherwise his boss would want to know why he didn't, but if he did so, wifey would find out that he had come and gone sometime in the afternoon without announcing himself. He couldn't leave it outside the house, after his employers' admonition. It was too risky for that even for such a safe area. He'd had a look at the piece of jewellery and reckoned that the market value had to be in the high four figure range at least.

He decided to take the risk. He owed Mr Big Shot some loyalty and he owed his wife nothing. Perhaps if she'd been possessed of a better attitude during their previous encounter he might have suffered a smidgen of remorse, but he had to make a choice. His unenviable task was made easier as suddenly the door of the room opened and the nude woman appeared clutching a smock. Her expression when she saw Devin standing there was one of complete disbelief.

She appeared to be trying to speak, although her lips were moving, so great was her obvious discomfort and shock, that no sound was forthcoming. Devin used the opportunity to get off the first shot. Placing the jewellery box on a table next to the door, he remarked "You don't look as if you need this right now, but it's going to look very attractive on you later." With that, he left the house as quickly as he could.

Coming back down the hill with the necessity of now having to return to the office to report on the situation, Devin was sweating bullets. My career at the agency is over, he thought - maybe he was being paid back for some unwise action he had unwittingly taken or some task he had neglected.

To say that his boss was surprised to see him was a massive understatement. However, he had no intention of becoming the victim of a trumped up version from the other side. To his immense relief, his story was accepted without the slightest hesitation. This was because, as he subsequently discovered, suspicions of infidelity had been on Mr Big Shot's mind for sometime. Therefore, instead of being hauled over the coals as he had expected, exactly the opposite happened. He was promoted the week after the incident to be an executive assistant, and was given an two hundred dollar per month raise. When the divorce case came to court on the grounds of adultery with at least three men, Devin was the star witness. The joke around the office for months - not within his earshot - was that he had been a lot cheaper than a private detective agency. From then on, he was on his way.

When the opportunity arose, three years later, by way of an offer from two Young Turks who were chafing under the supervision of their superiors at another agency, Devin decided to take a big step up the corporate ladder by joining them in opening their own boutique outfit. Being single and not being a gambler or wild spender, he had managed to accumulate a not unsubstantial nest egg, the greater part of which under the terms of his deal with the other two he was obliged to invest. The venture proved to be wildly successful due in no small part to the fact that he and his partners managed to entice several up and coming actors and actresses to follow them away from their respective previous places of representation. This phenomenon which is typical of the agency business unfortunately managed to generate a great deal of ill feeling with his partners' previous employers. Not only was this ignored, but one of his new colleagues cheekily put up a sign in his office which declared 'All's fair in love and war AND artist management!'.

When Devin had tried to express some regrets about leaving his firm, he was brusquely cut short by his soon to be ex-employer. "Always remember this," he said. "In Hollywood, never apologize for anything; saying sorry is seen as a sign of weakness." Many years later, Devin was reminded of this remark when a prominent English actor was seen on a nationally televised late night talk show expressing his regret for employing the sexual services of a prostitute just off Sunset Boulevard. His personality began to change, and his behavior in his efforts to promote his clients to studios and production companies became, on occasion, brusque and aggressive. This was by no means the exception to the rule in the agency world, but by the end of the 70's he had acquired the reputation of a character who took no prisoners and who preferred the tactics of confrontation to those of diplomacy as often as possible.

On the day of Lucy's appointment Devin was in a very good mood. He had by now stepped up his pursuit of desirable women to a much higher level than the secretarial types that he lusted after when employed with his previous agency. In fact, he had recently seduced an up and coming young actress who he had met at a showbiz party and had just returned the night before from a four day Colorado Springs trip with her. She had not yet joined his firm but Devin felt that it was only a matter of time. She was impressed that he did not pressure her on the change-over, and showed it, so he had every reason to feel smug about the situation.

He was intrigued that in Dan's message to him he had mentioned that the actress he was sending over was English. Earlier that morning one of his partners had mentioned a story in the Hollywood Reporter describing a sexual escapade at a Hollywood party the previous Friday. The article had noted that the incident involved an English actress and Devin wondered if there was any connection with his visitor.

Lucy entered his office hesitantly. She was dressed in a dark blue suit and was wearing flat shoes. Her long blonde hair was done up in a bun at the back of her head. The shoes were a good idea because she didn't have a car and she had taken the wrong bus which necessitated her walking six blocks to get to her destination. Devin was the perfect gentleman, getting up from behind his desk and helping her into a cushioned chair facing him. "Tell me about yourself," he began.

Lucy started by explaining her background in her native country and then described her circuitous path which had led her eventually to Southern California. When she was finished, Devin was quick to set her mind at ease by assuring her that although she had mentioned that she had never met Dan, he could assure her that he was a person of the highest integrity and that his recommendation was a huge plus in her favor. Meanwhile, his mind was going in another direction. He refrained from trying to satisfy his curiosity verbally as to why a producer would recommend an actress he had never met and whose work he had never seen, but there, he felt, had to be a reason which hopefully would reveal itself sooner rather than later. Lucy began to relax as the conversation developed and was visibly encouraged when Devin mentioned that he would be visiting the set in Las Vegas on Wednesday afternoon.

"Perhaps we could have some supper then," he explored in a overture which produced a friendly response. Thus encouraged, he began making mental plans to taking the relationship further. After all, why not?

He got out of his chair as if to say goodbye, but on an impulse, decided to escort her out of the building. Putting on the coat of his immaculately pressed Armani suit he declined the handshake offered.

"I'll come down with you. It'll only take a minute."

They rode the four floors down the elevator in silence. What a nice guy, Lucy thought, taking the time to see me out. Of course, this was the impression he had deliberately planned. It was not until they reached the glass-door exit to the street that Devin delivered the punch line.

"Of course, we'd be happy to provide representation for you. Are you a member of the Screen Actor's Guild?"

"Not yet, but I intend to join as soon as possible. Hopefully, if I get a role in this film, it'll make that possible."

"I'm sure it will. I'll personally help you with the paperwork. Then, almost as an afterthought as Lucy was going through the door, he added, "Do you have a Green Card?"

The question stopped Lucy in her tracks.

"Well, it was being arranged for me, but unfortunately I don't think I'll be seeing the guy that was doing that anymore."

Devin winked.

"Don't worry about that; I can arrange it. Not a problem."

CHAPTER 14

Monday night was a sleepless one for Peter. He had arrived back at his guest house half expecting to find Bard waiting for him. That's how paranoid he had become. Added to that was the image of Catherine's mother's distress. He wished that he had never visited the two women in West Hollywood. Too late to change that now; the only good news was that Lucy had left a message saying that the meeting with the agent had been very successful and that she looked forward to seeing him in Las Vegas. At least I've done something right, he thought. Perhaps it will all work out OK. He had not told his landlord that he was leaving the next morning but he had made sure that his rent was fully paid up. Although he was on a weekly rate, he was not legally obliged to give any advance notice that he was checking out. In other words, not exactly a 'moonlight flit'. On his way to catch the bus to the airport, he ducked into the Roosevelt Hotel and put a dime in a pay phone. Patricia sounded sleepy.

"Hello?"

"Hi, this is Peter. How are you?"

"Fine, I guess. What time is it?"

"It's 7:45 a.m. Sorry if I woke you but I'm leaving town this morning for a little while and I thought I should speak to you before I go. I'm glad I caught you."

"What about?" She asked curiously, wide awake by now.

Peter decided to answer the question by sidestepping it.

"Do you think that you could hang around for a little longer? There's something else that I didn't mention about your sister's death and I'd like to discuss it with you in person."

"Can't you tell me now?"

"Not really," Peter replied somewhat impatiently. "My plane is just about to take off" he prevaricated, "but it's something that's really important. I'll be back by the end of the week."

"Where are you going?"

"Well, I've got to do something for a living and I've been offered a Job on a film as a gofer in Nevada for a while. I'm hoping to get back on Sunday for a day. Perhaps we could meet then if you could stay that long."

"The inquest is on Wednesday and my mother wants to leave right after. We're flying Catherine's body back to Wisconsin for the funeral there unless we're denied permission for some reason. I can't let my mother travel on her own, it wouldn't be right. Could you let me have your new number?"

"I honestly don't have one yet. I'll call you by Sunday, I promise and I'll be able to give you the information by then at the latest."

Patricia persisted, "Can't you give me just a little hint what you're talking about?"

Before he had a chance to think about how to respond, Peter blurted out "I think I can give a positive ID to the police on the person responsible for your sister's death."

"That's not what you said yesterday. Please, please tell me what happened?" She was now sounding hysterical.

"I give you my word I'll tell you everything I know. I just can't talk anymore right now, I'll miss my plane. Please trust me, I will call you, I promise. I've got to go now. Bye"

Peter terminated the conversation with decidedly mixed feelings. He knew that she would relate the details to Bard and that the latter would really be after him now. On the other hand, he felt a sense of relief that he had made a major step in getting the matter off his chest. It had been troubling him for the last four days and its intensity had increased ever since his meeting with the two women.

He was right about nearly missing his flight. Red was waiting anxiously at the gate when Peter arrived breathlessly, having sprinted from the ticket counter. Fortunately, he only had a tote bag with him which his companion good-naturedly took hold of as they were about to embark. One day, Los Angeles would hopefully have a subway system, Peter thought, and maybe, just maybe, people on a budget would have a quicker way of getting to and from the airport.

As Red explained once they were airborne, the glory of descending onto the desert oasis could not be fully appreciated during the daytime. Nevertheless, the sensation of the ever increasing proximity of so many tall buildings appearing as part of a mega-fantasy after sixty minutes of flying over an arid area was the most exhilarating visual experience of Peter's entire life.

By coincidence, as his companion revealed, they and the rest of the film crew were going to be staying at The Riviera, the casino hotel owned by the husband of the young lady involved in the

Golden Globes controversy. Or was it really a coincidence, Peter wondered. After all, there were obviously many choices for accommodation. As for the producers and the 'above the line' personnel i.e. the stars of the film, the director and other key players, they would be booked in at Caesars Palace. According to Red, this was several blocks south on the Strip, as the main thoroughfare, Las Vegas Boulevard, was known. Caesars was, as its name implied, built to resemble a Roman Emperor's palace complete with a make believe Coliseum. There a legion of unlucky gamblers at the casino might feel that they had been thrown to the lions of yesteryear after their unsuccessful forays into the gambling den.

The sky was clear but the temperature was much chillier than in Los Angeles. Peter had taken Red's advice and had packed a heavy sweater for the night time which often went well below freezing point. Right now, he had something more important on his mind. He wanted to work off his debt to Eric by paying him back the $3,000, preferably in the same way he had been bribed: cold hard cash. First things first, though, Peter reasoned. He had been briefed by Red on the way to the hotel that there was to be a meeting with the producers over at Caesars at 6 p.m., followed by a cast and crew pre-production party scheduled to last until midnight. With shooting on location due to begin early the next morning, he doubted that it would last that late.

The plot of the film had two main points: the first dealt with the creation of Las Vegas as a gambling resort by the East Coast Mafia and how the chief architect of the project who while in many ways a visionary was suspected of stealing from his financiers, while at the same time adopting a hedonistic lifestyle. Unfortunately, he had paid the ultimate price in a Beverly Hills house not very far from the palatial home where Peter had begun his odyssey on the previous Friday. The second part dealt with the infiltration by these financiers and their cohorts into the Nevada gambling industry.

The two stars in real life were known amongst their peers to have extremely opposite characteristics. The male lead continuously received nothing but respect in every aspect of his life both on screen and off, but to a large extent, because of his choice of esoteric roles, had achieved nowhere near the box-office success that his talent deserved. The female star had also achieved worthy acclaim, but her background before entering the industry was cloaked in ambiguity. According to Dan, she had the reputation of being a demanding diva and included in her contract on this film were complicated clauses covering an exceptionally wide range. Good examples of this were an insistence of no nudity, gratuitous or otherwise, to the specific type of bottled water and brand of coffee that had to be always available to her in her trailer, or in her dressing room on indoor locations. As for the director, it was doubtful whether a more intelligent choice could have been made, again according to Dan. Two years previously, the director and the male lead had combined to create one of the most critically praised features of the decade.

After Peter had arrived at the hotel he decided to surprise Lucy by knocking on her door after getting her room number from Red who had the list of the cast and crew's living arrangements. This way he would experience her spontaneous reaction rather than if she had known he was coming to visit.

"Who is it?"

"It's me. Are you fully clothed?"

"Who's me?" asked Lucy who opened the door at the same time anyway.

"PETER!!!"with the scream barely out of her mouth she responded the way her visitor hoped she would by throwing herself at him, wrapping her arms around him and hugging him.

"Thank you, thank you, thank you, thank you!"

"Oh don't worry about it. I didn't really do a lot, it's Dan Johnson you should thank; he set the whole thing up."

"Yeah, but if you hadn't asked him to help, it would never have happened."

He looked at the figure in front of him. With her hair in a ponytail, a well scrubbed face devoid of any makeup, wearing a red tank top and white shorts, Lucy looked like a hot college student. She also looked more attractive than ever. She moved across the room and sat on the bed. He found it difficult to resist the urge to join her but he needed to take this opportunity to set the record straight.

"You know that night we met, I'd just had the most dramatic day of my life."

"What do you mean, Peter?"

"Well, you told me all about yourself when we came back to your apartment..."

"I don't remember too much about that," Lucy interrupted. "Anyway, there's not much I want to remember."

Peter nodded in sympathy. Sitting down beside her on the bed, he gently took her hand in his.

"You told me in great detail about your life and how you happened to end up in Los Angeles."

"Drifted west by circumstance?"

Peter laughed. "Yes, you could say that. Anyway, I was happy that you instinctively trusted me enough to confide in me."

"I must have been more drunk than I thought."

They both laughed.

"Well, it's my turn to repay the compliment."

With this introduction, Peter related the story of events that began the previous Friday. He spoke non-stop for half an hour leaving out any reference to Eric's involvement in the death at the motel, explaining that he had met him at a party. Lucy listened patiently, her only response being occasionally raised eyebrows and in two instances, open mouthed astonishment but she made absolutely no sound whatever during his lengthy narrative until he stopped speaking.

"It's incredible. To think that all that has happened to you in just four days."

"Yes, and it's not over yet. Not by any stretch of the imagination. I've got to find a way to get the detective off my back; I just know he doesn't buy my story. I just know it. That's the main reason I took this job, to get away from the heat."

Peter looked at Lucy's face to see any sign of disbelief, but there was none. Suitably encouraged, he continued.

"Come to think of it, I don't really know what I'll be doing here. All I've done so far is run a couple of errands for which I've been paid pretty well. I expect I'm going to be used some sort of gofer, although Eric said he's going to give me a little part in the movie."

"Well I'm much in the same boat myself. I don't know anything about my role in the film, whatever it may be. The agent I saw is coming over on Wednesday from L.A. That might help."

"How'd you get on with him?"

"Okay, I guess. He's kind of pushy but that's probably par for the course. He wants to take me to dinner when he gets here."

"So long as you're not on the dessert menu." Peter smirked.

Lucy shrugged.

"That thought did cross my mind too. I guess I'll have to see how it goes. Perhaps I'll be working and will have to break the date," she chuckled.

Outside the sunshine was fading rapidly and as if on cue, the multicoloured lights of the casinos were beginning to be illuminated rather like lures meant to attract the hordes of unsuspecting visitors into their web. The pair sat silently on the bed gazing out of the window onto the Strip as if in a trance mesmerized by the ever changing spectacle that was unfolding before their eyes. For a first time visitor to Vegas, the panorama of neon being created at twilight is unique and is an impression which will linger in the memory for ever.

It was Lucy who broke the silence. Placing her lips gently to Peter's ear as if she was unwilling to have her words overheard, she whispered "How much time do we have?"

Peter was just a little bit slow on the uptake.

"What….." he hesitated, "What do you mean?"

"How much time before we have to be at the party?" It was then that the penny dropped "About an hour."

Moving swiftly, Lucy unbuckled Peter's belt and unzipped his trousers, expertly her hand found its way to his rapidly stiffening cock and firmly pulled it out. He didn't resist although he could not get it out of his head that the timing may have been less than perfect.

Kicking off his shoes and socks, he pulled down his trousers and in a second her mouth was devouring him. She paused momentarily to reassure him.

"Relax. As you know I have experience in this category." she said as she hurriedly pulled off her tank top to reveal her firm pert breasts.

Peter helped remove her shorts. She was travelling commando, not wearing any knickers.

His erect cock readily responded to her enthusiastic efforts. After what seemed like no time at all, she was straddling him, rising and falling with urgency indicative of someone with no time to lose. They climaxed in unison as darkness fell, the vivid colors of the external rainbow reflecting on the windows of the room as if joining in their sexual celebration.

CHAPTER 15

Riding up the Strip now totally bathed in extravagant hues, with Red at the wheel, Peter could not help but reflect on the irony of his present situation. From leading a one dimensional life as a motel clerk at the beck and call of a Korean who even charged his employees if they should ever need to stay overnight, his revised position now found him conditioned by a new ambiance of luxury and glamor. The colors bouncing off the limo windows were the external factors, while the influence of the characters who had invaded his space were clashing entitities which all occupied his immediate attention. Lucy remained silently by his side as if in increasing apprehension of what lay in store for her. Red chose the opportunity to fill in some of the gaps in their new surroundings.

"This is a great place to buy an expensive watch, like a Rolex, real cheap. So many gamblers find themselves out of cash, in some cases very suddenly, that they part with expensive possessions at ridiculously low prices when they would never do the same thing back home where they come from."

"What's your opinion on gambling, Red?" asked Peter suddenly. "Is it a disease, or just a hobby that sometimes gets out of control?"

"Let me put it this way; do you see that casino over there?" said Red, pointing to the Flamingo Hotel and Casino which they just about to pass..

"That's where it all started. Bugsy Siegel came here in 1947 with the idea of creating a gambling oasis here in the desert and this is where he pitched his tent. I already told you what happened to him, but look around you. There's a huge amount of money left behind by the millions of people who come here, making the casino owners very rich. In short, if you build it they will come."

"Nice turn of phrase."

"Yeah, it will probably be used in a movie one day, and I won't get the credit for it. The story I just told you, as you know, is basically what Eric and Dan's movie is about."

The limo pulled into Caesars Palace and disappeared into the parking structure. Entering the casino by way of an elevator was a revelation to Peter. Far bigger than his accommodation down the Strip, he was staggered by the size of his new surroundings. Above all the noise, the clanging of slot machines monopolized his attention as the trio made their way to the front desk. This was reached by way of a long corridor with restaurants on one side and a nightclub in the shape of a huge galleon on the other. So this was the Temple of Mammon which Warren Beatty and Elizabeth Taylor had frolicked in front of in the 1970 movie The Only Game In Town, crystallizing itself forever after in his young mind as the epitome of over indulgence.

"We're here for the film party" announced Red grandly as if the receptionist would know exactly what he was talking about. The woman immediately picked up her phone and within a couple of minutes two individuals looking like refugees from a Hollywood film set dressed, not exactly unsurprisingly, considering the casino theme, as Caesar and Cleopatra, appeared by their sides. Caesar courteously took Lucy's hand and beckoned her with his other arm toward the far end of the cavernous lounge, motioning for us to follow. Cleopatra took Red and myself by the arm and urged us both forward so as not to be left behind. Our entourage travelled at least fifty yards along winding corridors until the noise of voices grew louder with each step until we arrived at our destination. A large bronze handled pair of doors were 'manned' by two gorgeous women albeit dressed in a more contemporary style with a banner announcing the event above reading "BLACK JACK FILM PARTY".

We've made it, thought Peter. Obviously a little late because the party was in full swing, but we're here. Red excused himself, perhaps to let Eric know that everything was in order. The two youngsters were suddenly on their own in the midst of a babbling inferno of chatter. Peter decided that the best thing to do was to get a drink for both of them and he led Lucy over to one of the bar stations. Eric spotted the couple and came over.

"Is this a great party or what? I don't know about you two, but I'm having a super time."

"Do you remember Lucy?"

"But of course. I want both of you to come and meet the director right now because he's threatening to go to bed, the silly fellow."

Eric looked as if he had a few drinks, but not so much that would make him incoherent. Nevertheless he was a bit unsteady on his feet as he led the way over to a small group where a slender fortysomething man dressed in a casual blazer and blue jeans was talking away nineteen to the dozen. Peter stood respectfully to one side as Eric waited for the right moment to interrupt his rapid monologue which was hard to decipher so speedily were the words coming out of his mouth. Eventually he paused to catch his breath and Eric seized his chance.

"Julio, I'd like you to meet my assistant, Peter and my young protégée, Lucy."

The director who was short and slender with a pencil moustache shook hands and turned to Eric in an animated way "I'm glad you came back. I'm leaving in five minutes. Will you be with us tomorrow morning?"

"Yes I will."

"At six am?"

"Yes, for sure"

"Then you should go to bed now, as well "

Peter wasn't sure if this was a wish, or a demand but decided it wasn't any of his business anyway. Turning to the young couple, the director smiled politely .

"Good to meet you. Please excuse me, I have to say good-bye to some people. Eric, I see you then."

"Of course."

After he had departed, Eric grabbed Peter by the arm and whispered conspiratorially into his ear.

"I'm not going anywhere near that set at 6 a.m tomorrow but I never had any intention of telling him. I have something I want you to do for me later. Can you come to my suite 1869 in half an hour?"

"Sure. I'll find it."

Turning to Lucy, Eric gestured "Dan wants to meet you. Peter, why don't you take her over and do the introductions. He's over at the table in the corner." pointing in that direction.

Peter pushed his way through the throng with Lucy at his side. His mind was now occupied with what Eric needed him for but he had to try to concentrate on the matter at hand. Fortunately, Dan had spoken to Devin late on Monday and as soon as he saw Lucy approaching, a flicker of recognition crossed his face.

"My dear, you are as beautiful as everyone has insisted."

Lucy immediately felt at ease with this man. Whatever tentative thoughts had occupied her mind about the forthcoming meeting vanished as the conversation progressed and Dan's affability had a calming effect on her. She had been worried that her notoriety after the incident on the previous Friday night would disqualify her from being taken seriously by her benefactor, but she soon became completely at ease in his company. Waving aside her expression of gratitude, Dan declared "I can't promise you a lot, but you're definitely going to be on screen in this production. We'll sort out all the details with Devin when he comes over from LA tomorrow evening."

"What about the director? Did he make any comments when you mentioned me?"

"This picture has been cast even down to the small parts, but there's no way that I'm going to renege on my promise to you. The kid stays in the picture."

Dan laughed at his own reference to the famous remark allegedly made by Darryl Zanuck when he insisted that the part of Robert Evans as a bull fighter in The Sun Also Rises would not be edited out of *that* movie.

"Thank you. I really appreciate it."

"Don't mention it. Now if you'll excuse me, I have to make a couple of important phone calls so I'm going to go to my suite. If you need me for anything, leave a message at reception"

Peter and Lucy circulated around the party for a while and were eventually joined by Red after he was finished doing whatever it was he had to do. At least Lucy would be able to get a ride back down the Strip, Peter thought. Making his excuses to her, explaining that there was some urgent business that he had to attend to and promising to call her later, he retraced his steps out of the ballroom. Going back through the lobby, he could see increased activity in the casino as the night time crowd began to multiply in size. How many of these people would lose their shirts tonight, he wondered. The nickname of the city as 'Lost Wages' seemed totally appropriate. Taking the elevator up to Eric's suite, he decided that he would use the opportunity to seize the initiative and press his patron to give him a precise account of what his duties were and what kind of salary he could expect.

Hopefully, he would accumulate the amount of Eric's bribe as soon as possible so that he would not have this continuingly nagging feeling of indebtedness hanging over him much longer. When he arrived, Eric got straight to the point.

"I need your help tomorrow night. The position is that myself, Dan and Tommy plus our director and the two principal actors are all staying here at Caesars while the rest of the cast and the more important members of the crew are booked in at the Riviera. However, I have a deal with the management here that all our rooms are 'comped'.

131

This means that we don't pay for them providing at least one of us plays at the high stakes blackjack or roulette tables for a certain amount of hours every day of our stay. The casino knows that I'm a heavy blackjack gambler or as the expression goes, 'high roller'. As soon as I sit down, I hand in a 'players' card and the pit boss will check to see how long I play at the tables. The system is called being 'rated'. Of course, they hope I will lose - I know that - but they would never admit it."

"Why do you need to get the rooms free? Peter asked "Doesn't the production company cover this in the budget?"

"Well," said Eric rubbing his cheek and motioning Peter to sit down, "To be honest, we are a little under funded on the budget of this film and any financial relief would be welcome. Because I play blackjack for high stakes, I get a 'marker', or credit, before I start gambling which I sign for. If I lose, obviously I have to settle up with the casino. But if I win, which is as far as most people are concerned, is the whole point of gambling, I cash in my chips and I get paid the difference between my winnings and the marker. I have to play every night to keep the comp going and this is where you would be very useful to me. I need a certain amount of cash everyday for various payments related to the filming, so here's the deal. When I'm at the blackjack table, I need you to be nearby because every so often I am going to get up to go to the men's room. This is the signal for you follow me a minute later so I can pass over some chips to you to take to the cashier in exchange for money. Don't stand too near the table as you will arouse suspicion."

Peter understood what was required of him but he was troubled that Eric wanted to engage him in still more devious behavior.

"Isn't this illegal?"

Eric laughed. "Well…, not exactly. I'm not actually stealing from the casino, I'm just not returning their loan at the appropriate time. I wouldn't worry too much about it; casinos have plenty of money. I'm trying to get myself out of a temporary jam, that's all."

Once again, another irony for Peter. The game of blackjack was being used to help solve a problem arising on the production of a film of the same name. Life imitating Art possibly?

"I don't mind doing this for you," Peter prevaricated, "but why don't you ask Red? He's been here lots of times and I'm sure his experience could be very helpful"

"Not really. You're young, good looking and you blend in with the surroundings. I'll make arrangements tomorrow morning to have you dressed appropriately. In any event, Red is going to be busy tomorrow night with transportation matters."

"What exactly would I be doing here in Vegas apart from this, Eric? We really haven't discussed this, have we?" asked Peter anxiously.

"No, we haven't. And the reason for this is that I'm not in a mind to give you a precise title. To make you feel better about the deal, I'll give you a five per cent cut of the money we'll get from your cashing the chips. Would that be okay with you?"

Once again, Peter was of the opinion that he had been given a Brandoesque offer that he couldn't refuse. I wonder how long it will take for me to make some money legitimately, he thought. Perhaps I'm no different from all the gamblers here in Vegas who are trying to get something for nothing and I don't even realize it.

CHAPTER 16

Bard looked at his fingernails with disgust. That's what frustration does to you, he thought sardonically. The job can eat at your heart and soul but it provides food by way of your fingernails first. He was doing some paperwork at the station when the call came through. It was from Lopez. A man who closely resembled Chester's mug shot had been spotted with another guy in a car travelling South on Robertson and they were giving chase with the siren on. Bard almost leapt out of his chair in excitement.

"Don't lose him!" he bellowed. "I don't want that son of a bitch getting away this time." He raced out of the room scattering papers as he went and took the stairs two at a time down to the parking lot. His car roared out the gate with the driver's side door swinging back and forth until he slammed it shut. Keeping in radio contact with his colleague, he sped down Highland toward Pico on which street Chester had just turned East. With a bit of luck and help from traffic lights, he would meet him almost head on unless the suspect managed to give the patrol car the slip by turning onto a side street.

Bard got to Pico just in time to see the black and white blaze past. Swinging left, he followed right behind at about eighty miles an hour. It was just after midnight on a Tuesday, slow for traffic at that time but the streets were not totally empty, a fact that Chester and his companion would regret. Their car bounced off a blue-colored bus and crashed into a fence just before Normandie.

Chester kicked open the door on the passenger side of the severely damaged Toyota and tried to make a run for it. This time he was not so lucky as he was sacked quarterback style by Lopez's partner Hernandez while the other officer, gun drawn, approached the driver who was slumped over the wheel.. Bard rushed over a few moments later to the struggling would be escapee and jammed his right foot squarely on Chester's neck.

"Move and I'll break it." Bard growled as Hernandez completed the cuffing procedure. With his captive safely in the back seat of the patrol car, they both joined Lopez who was attempting to lift the driver out of the car. He appeared to be unconscious and was bleeding from a head wound.

"Call paramedics". Bard instructed.

"10-4"

"Come with me, Hernandez. Lopez can wait - on second thought I'll take the prisoner back to Wilcox. When you come back, file the report and leave it on my desk."

"Okay Lieutenant." Everybody called Bard 'Lieutenant' even though he was still a Sergeant.

Bard felt like a man who had been given a second chance at life. He pulled Chester out of the black and white and shoved him into the back of his own car.

"So, Chester, we meet again. So soon. How unlucky for you."

"Fuck you, man."

Bard leaned over to the back seat and delivered a solid right hand to Chester's face.

"Whaddya say?" asked Bard in his New York twang. "I didn't hear you so good."

Chester howled in pain, "Why'd you do that man,? You just broke my nose."

"That's right. You were resisting arrest so I had to deal with you."

"What...?"

"Shut up, not another peep out of you till we get to the station. Then, maybe, MAYBE, I might just read you your Miranda - if I'm in a good mood."

Chester started to say something, then thought better of it.

"You've given me a lot of trouble so don't expect any favors."

Chester nodded. "Okay man. You win."

"It's not about winning, jerk. It's about getting scum like you off the street and into the pen."

Bard drove up Western from Pico, glancing from time to time in the rear view mirror at his prisoner.

"Tell me, Mr Clever Dick. What do you actually do for a living?:

"Well, I'm in between jobs right now."

"Translation; your hooker split and you haven't pimped your way onto another one yet, right?"

"No man, that's not the way it is."

"Oh, I see. You just decided to go into another line of business. What were you doing driving around with Blondie?"

"Oh, he's from out of town. A mutual friend hooked us up."

"I guess he was trying to improve race relations," Bard snorted. "Don't lie to me, Chester. If we find any dope on either of you or in the car, you're going to be in more trouble. No, scratch that. You're in deep shit now anyway, so it couldn't get much worse."

"I haven't done anything."

"If you haven't done anything, why were you running away? Not once, twice."

Bard swung onto Wilcox from Santa Monica Boulevard and turned into the station. Pulling Chester out of the vehicle, he took a handkerchief out of his pocket and cleaned his face up on their way into the building. Inside, Bard escorted him over to the Sergeant's desk.

"Book him on evading arrest on suspicion of felony. I need to question him before I decide what else to charge him with. There's more I need to know."

"Okay Lieutenant. Looks like he didn't come quietly." To Chester, "Do you need a doctor?"

Chester shrugged, "No I don't think so."

As the detective was going down the hallway, the officer called out to him. "Oh, by the way, there's a woman here to see you. Says she works at the motel where the homicide took place on Friday."

"Very good. Tell her I'll see her in ten minutes. I've got some paperwork I need to attend to." Bard walked through the center of the room and into his office. After a short interval, there was a knock on the half open door.

"Come in."

Lupe slowly entered the room, obviously very nervous. A petite individual dressed in a flowered blouse and a green skirt with black hair tied in a knot on the back of her head, she hesitated in front of Bard's desk. He motioned to her to sit down.

"I remember you. We took a statement from you Friday didn't we?"

"Yes but I ..." Lupe's voice trailed off.

Bard was quick to see her apprehension and realizing that she may have something important to say, tried to make her feel at ease.

"Please make yourself comfortable. I want you to know I very much appreciate your coming in to see me. How can I help you?"

Lupe tried to compose herself as if she was not at all sure that being there was such a good idea. Bard went over to the water cooler and poured her a cup.

"It's okay. Don't be afraid."

"This is the first time I been in a police station."

"Is that right?"

"Yes. It's not so nice."

"No it isn't. Most people who come here don't want to."

"I went to mass on Sunday and in confession, my priest advised that I come see you."

Bard got the distinct feeling that he was just about to hear a crucial piece of new information.

"Yes, and..."

He waited expectantly.

"I must tell you now you didn't get whole story on Friday."

"Who from?"

"From the clerk."

"Peter?"

"Yes."

"What do you mean?"

"The man in 210 with the girl..."

Lupe was finding it difficult to finish the sentence.

"Yes?"

"He was a white man, about fifty."

"Are you sure?"

"I very sure. Yes, I very very sure. I was cleaning rooms and Peter told me to go to 210 to make certain everything ready. I was just coming out when I saw this man with key. He opened door and went in. When I came down after one hour I said nothing because Peter, he must have given key to this man."

"So, what happened then?"

"I don't know because I was cleaning room on second floor at back. Friday is very busy day, but not Saturday or Sunday so I was trying to finish by my time to leave at four. Next thing I know is that Peter said he called police and you came and asked me some questions."

"I remember."

Bard looked at some papers on his desk.

"Your name is Lupe Villasenor, correct?"

"Yes"

"Do you know the black guy that was in the motel on Friday afternoon?"

"You mean Chester?"

"Aah, you know Chester. Very good. Yes that's the one."

"Everybody know Chester. He come to motel all the time. He is, as we say, prohibido, but he come anyway. He don't seem to care. Yes he was in motel earlier, but I don't think in that room. No, definitely not."

"Can I find you at the motel if I need you?"

"Yes. No problem. I work there for two years now."

"Okay. I may need you soon. Thank you for coming in."

As Lupe got up to go, Hernandez came into the room with a written report of the evening's episode.

"Just the man I want to see. I need you and Lopez to go round to that guest house on Las Palmas and get that motel guy, Harris, in for questioning. He's surely got to be home by now. Can you do that for me right away?"

"Okay lieutenant. We're on our way."

Lopez cursed softly when he heard about the extra chore. He had the day off on Wednesday and was hoping to leave the station as soon as possible so that he could get a good night's sleep. He had promised to take his wife and young son to Disneyland at 8 a.m. so that they could spend the whole day there to celebrate her birthday. Rubber burned as the black and white screamed up Wilcox and made a left turn onto Hollywood Boulevard. Arriving at the Las Palmas address Lopez confronted the night clerk.

"He's not here anymore, he checked out," the man informed the officer matter of factly.

"When was that?"

"Apparently sometime this morning."

"Any forwarding address?"

"You know something, he didn't even tell anyone he was definitely leaving. The day manager went up to see him about this week's rent and the room was empty apart from a couple of things that he left behind."

"Can we take a look?"

"I guess so. The maid was sick today so the room hasn't been made up yet. Here's the key. It's the third from the end out the back on the second floor."

"Thanks. This won't take long. My chief's not going to be happy about this - he wants to see him right away."

"I don't think that's gonna happen."

Upstairs, a quick glance around the sparsely furnished room yielded no information. On the way out Lopez checked the trash can by the door. Crumpled up inside was a brochure for Las Vegas casinos. Underneath the name Caesars Palace the phone number was circled in ink. He stuck it in his pocket and went downstairs. The clerk was watching TV and as they passed he remarked; "This might help you. I remember that he got a message last night that he needed to catch a bus outside the Roosevelt Hotel at 7:30 a.m. this morning."

Back at Wilcox, Bard was informed about this development. He was about to leave for the night when the phone rang. A voice sounding very relieved was on the other end.

"I've been trying to reach you all day."

"Who's this?"

"This is Tricia Mack, Catherine's sister. I got a call from Peter the clerk at the Best Inn this morning. I thought you ought to know what he said. He admitted that he knew something about my sister's death that he's not told anyone about yet"

" Did he say what it was?"

"No, unfortunately not"

"What else did he say?"

"Not much. I wanted him to explain, but he said that he couldn't. Not then, anyway. He was at the airport. He said he was rushing to catch a plane to go work on a film."

"Did he way where he was going?" Bard continued.

"No." .

"Can you think of anything at all that indicated his plans?" Bard's voice betrayed the urgency that was now enveloping him.

"I wish I could."

"Could it have something to do with Las Vegas?" Bard was looking at the pamphlet that the detective had put on his desk.

"I don't know, really I don't."

"What time was this?"

"Around 8:30 a.m.."

"Thanks. I'll get back to you."

Bard put down the phone and immediately called LAX. Identifying himself, he inquired, "Do you have any flights to Las Vegas between 8:30 and 9 a.m.?"

"Yes sir, would you like a reservation? I'll put you through."

"No, not right now, but I do have another question. Do you have any other flights to Nevada leaving at that time?"

"Just a moment." After several seconds, the voice came back on the phone, "No sir, not from this airport."

"Thank you. You've been very helpful." Click.

CHAPTER 17

Devin had reserved a room at MGM Ballys for a specific reason. He was fully aware that Dan and Eric along with the principal talent were staying across the street at Caesars and he preferred to keep his distance from them. This way his meeting with Lucy for dinner in his hotel that evening would go unnoticed. He could see Dan later. He had taken an afternoon flight from LA so that he could arrive in time to take a nap and get ready for the 9 p.m. rendezvous. As he was walking through McCarran Airport, Red came up to him.

"I spotted you right away. How are you?"

"Good. What's the latest news?"

"Eric and Tommy are up to something, but I'm not sure what it is yet."

"Well, keep your eyes open and let me know any developments. By the way, make sure you get that young lady over to my hotel in time for our meeting."

"You're the boss."

Devin proved to be a complete gentleman over dinner and when it was time for her to leave, he passed on a very substantial piece of advice.

"Look," he said, "I know what happened up at the party at David's house on Friday night. Everyone was talking about it on Monday. The important thing is not to dwell on it. Other things will soon take its place as a topic of conversation in Hollywood. In this country everyone deserves a second chance unless they've committed an unforgivable crime and your behavior could hardly be described as that. Dan has given you a couple of lines in the film and he and the screenwriter are going to go through them with you tomorrow. Where are you heading after this?"

"I'm not sure. My friend Peter has to help Eric out with something at Caesars and he asked me to join him there.. How long are you here for?"

"I'm going back tomorrow, unless you'd like me to stay longer," Devin replied, giving her a very long look.

Lucy didn't know how to respond to that not so veiled remark, so she didn't.

Devin pretended not to notice. "I'm glad you enjoyed your steak. It's very refreshing to see an actress with a good appetite. I certainly encourage it. Too many agents and managers insist that their clients lose weight even if they're thin enough already because they allegedly would have a better chance at landing the plum parts. I don't think Ava Gardiner or Kim Novak or even Grace Kelly lost any roles by having a full figure and the same goes now for Jane Fonda and Faye Dunaway."

Lucy decided to change the subject.

"What are you doing tomorrow?"

"Well, I have a meeting with Dan that's likely to last all morning. I'll be going over some business matters with him. As far as your lines are concerned, I think they'll be enough to get you a Screen Actor's Guild card."

"Thanks."

"No problem. It means that you'll get a check for sure."

Suddenly he lowered his voice. "I don't know if I should really tell you this so please don't mention it to anyone. I have clear proof that Eric has been stealing from Dan for some time and I've brought some evidence with me to show him when we meet tomorrow."

"How could that be possible?" Lucy asked unbelievingly.

"It's called 'creative accounting' and it happens all the time in Hollywood. For example, it's common knowledge in the business that a fellow countryman of yours who is a co-writer of one of the most successful television series of all time has been robbed blind by the producers for years and he only found out about it three months ago.

This is basically how it's been happening in this instance: Eric's production company is the registered owner of this project and he has the arrangement with Paramount to distribute the picture that is being made here. Dan's position is that he has controlling interest in the partnership by virtue of a separate legal agreement with Eric. He has invested heavily in many similar projects produced by the company and as such receives an executive producer's fee. However, in this capacity, Dan has certain legal obligations for which he is responsible including talent's salary. Eric has been padding the payroll with fictitious employees and passing all of that liability on to Dan. I'm not sure if his accountant has spotted it or not, but I certainly did. When I started in this business I learned all the tricks of the trade from one of the sharpest guys I have ever met, or am likely to meet in my entire life. As managers of our clients' money, for which we are obviously responsible we have to make damn certain that they don't get ripped off".

Lucy eyes widened in astonishment as Devin continued.

"When I worked for that guy, I learned pretty quickly that if the agent got ripped off he would run the risk of losing the client through financial incompetence or carelessness. Even though I'm pretty clued up myself, it never ceases to amaze me about the things producers do to deduct from the agreed fee for a client, particularly the less important members of the cast who always need the money the most. One of the things these guys do is what Eric is doing here, namely inventing cast members who don't exist and pocketing their salaries. Anyway, I want Dan to know the situation before the film gets fully under way and then we can discuss how to deal with this particular problem which incidentally I only discovered late last week."

"So you don't think much of Eric as a person, right?"

"You could say that. I can tell you right now what my main problem is going to be. Dan is going to find it difficult to believe that a business partner he's been associated with for a long time has been behaving dishonestly towards him. That's the way he is. I'm going to show him that the budget for the last two films that he and Eric have produced together have vastly inflated production costs to Dan's detriment. The reason I can do that is because I hired an independent auditor who has gone through the books with a fine tooth comb. He only handed in his report to me last week. For example, Eric's publicist, Tommy is contracted to earn a salary of $50,000 for 1979 but in the company's bank statement he found checks paid to her for just over

$150,000 in total. There's at least $100,000 unaccounted for on this item alone for which Dan is fifty percent liable. Quite frankly, I don't trust Tommy either –I'm sure she knows what's going on."

Devin looked at his watch He hoped that by divulging confidential information to Lucy, her trust in him would increase.

"You'd better go now. It takes a little while to cross over from here to Caesars. One day the people in charge of this town will build a bridge across this particular intersection so that car traffic can be avoided. It's the busiest spot in Vegas."

Devin saw her disappear into the crowded casino on her way out. One day, he thought. But not now. He had more important business to attend to now. Going to a pay phone, he called the hotel where Red was staying. He probably wouldn't be back for a while because he had driven Lucy up the Strip to meet him and he had a couple of errands to run, but he would leave a message for him to call Ballys later for last minute instructions. Red was important to Devin, because, with a foot in Eric's camp, any information on the latter's schemes would be more than extremely useful. As Dan's agent and manager he felt no twinge of conscience whatsoever paying Red for his services - his job was to protect his client's interests to the best of his ability, particularly when he knew for a fact that he was being taken advantage of..

* * * * *

148

Peter was relieved that Lucy had agreed to come along with him after he had relayed to her what Eric had required him to do.. He had a bad feeling about the whole operation and although he didn't really understand Eric's motives, he knew enough to realize that he was being asked to collect cash for gambling chips which were part of a debt to the casino. When Peter had asked if Lucy could come along that evening, Eric was only too happy to have her involved – her presence would provide even better cover for his scheme. When he joined up with his young accomplices at the appointed meeting place outside the casino buffet, his instructions to Peter were straight forward.

"I'll give you chips from time to time as if they are for you to go and gamble with. Every time I do that, that's the signal for you to go to the cashier's area and cash them in. After about twenty minutes come back to the blackjack table where I'm playing with a blank look on your face. I'll say something like 'have you had any luck' to which you will reply in the negative. Try a little grin when you say that. It'll make you look more human. If I don't say anything more at that time, it'll mean I don't have any more to give you right away. Go off somewhere else in the area and come back in another half an hour and so on and so on. I'm trying to raise fifty grand in cash tonight so obviously I'll be hoping to give you a lot of chips. Got all that?" Lucy and Peter nodded in unison.

" Let's do it"

"What happens if you lose everything?" Lucy asked.

"Well, we'll have to try again tomorrow night, won't we?" Eric responded with a grin.

With that philosophical remark, the couple followed Eric to the blackjack area where he sat down at the hundred dollar minimum table and asked for a 'marker' of $5,000. Eric signed the receipt that the pit boss gave him, the dealer counted fifty hundred dollar chips and he began to play. He chose the two end boxes with hardly any acknowledgment to the dealer.

At first he was scrutinized intently by the supervisor, standing to one side but Eric played conservatively and once the pit boss saw he wasn't a card counter as a few professional blackjack players are known to be, or indulge in any other type of suspicious behavior, he was more or less left unobserved. The two other players at the table, both males, seemed to be more interested in Lucy than the cards that they were being dealt, much to Eric's amusement.

Peter had never seen the game before but he quickly grasped the principle, namely that the gambler had to get a higher combination numerically than the 'house' without going over 21. For the first half an hour Eric seemed unable to win or lose very much; first of all he would be four or five hundred dollars in front and then about the same amount in the loss department. Peter began to feel bored, while Lucy, for her part, excused herself to go to the Ladies room, came back for a few minutes and then wandered off again. Peter wished he could join her but he had committed himself to what, so far, was the equivalent of watching grass grow.

Suddenly Eric started to win the battle with the dealer and rapidly accumulated a profit of $15,000 in white thousand dollar chips. At the prearranged signal, Peter approached the table and was discreetly given white chips to the value of $10,000. How did he know for sure, Peter thought that I wouldn't just disappear. After all, he didn't know me that well. However he was obviously a pretty good judge of character because I had no intention whatsoever of doing that. The transaction itself was facilitated by the arrival of a new dealer at the table which as Eric knew very well regularly happens at any table game in a casino when a gambler suddenly starts winning, particularly when the stakes are high. This allows the house to 'burn' a card, by taking a card from the shoe and putting it in the pack of used cards.

This is standard procedure on a dealer changeover and theoretically changes the gambler's luck as the winning sequence is disturbed. Peter was encouraged by this development. If Eric's luck continued he might be able to earn back the original $3,000 bribe and he only hoped that he could make his peace with Bard when the day of reckoning would arrive as it surely would very soon. A short period of time after changing the money he returned to the table. Eric had resumed his pattern of going two steps forward and two steps back metaphorically for the next hour. Then tragedy struck. In about five minutes he was virtually wiped out. A couple of unlucky doubledowns (doubling the chips on the table as a legitimate maneuver) with a lot of money at stake, splitting threes four times in one hand and doubling two of those again with the dealer getting twenty-one from three cards on both occasions and bingo, he needed more ammunition.

Peter anxiously noticed this dramatic turn of events and followed Eric as he got up from the table. The latter waved him off and proceeded to make his way to the cashier's cage. This was a large half moon shaped counter with faux-gold bars placed vertically at three inch intervals on the top of a shiny black marble counter.

"Yes sir, how can we help you?" The pale person with tinted glasses behind the bars inquired.

"My name is Eric Dagle and I'm staying here in the hotel."

"Yes?" The man responded, waiting for Eric to continue.

"I wish to acquire a marker for $5,000. Would that be possible?"

"Just a moment sir. This won't take very long."

With that the black suited bean-counter disappeared through a mirrored door into a back room, the interior of which was invisible from the outside of the cage. After more than a minute, more like five in fact, the man reappeared and confronted Eric at close quarters.

"I've had a word with my superior," as if it were perfectly normal to take ten minutes to have a word, "and he has instructed me to tell you, sir, that you have reached your limit."

"What limit?" a visibly annoyed Eric retorted. "Who says I have no more credit?"

"My manager, sir; would you like to speak with him?"

"You bet your sweet ass I'd like to speak with him. NOW!!"

Eric had by this time become visibly agitated and his voice had risen a few decibels. Peter watched the drama unfolding from a brief distance and noticed that other people were becoming aware of the confrontation. The flunky disappeared again and Eric began pacing up and down in front of the cage, muttering to himself and clenching and unclenching his fists. He was giving a good impression of a man who was doing his best to wear out the carpet he was treading on as quickly as possible.

An older man appeared from out of the side door of the inner office. He was short, shorter than Eric, somewhat bulky and wearing a gray suit with a black tie. He had an unhealthy pallor to his skin which is not unusual for people who work in casinos and appeared to be in his sixties, but he gave Peter the impression that he looked as if he could take care of himself if the occasion arose. He walked slowly toward Eric.

"Mr. Dagle?" he inquired softly.

"Yes" hissed Eric.

"I'm the casino manager on duty this shift and my name is William Glugt. My decision on this matter is that your line of credit has been maximized and you're not in a position to receive another marker from us tonight. I need hardly remind you……"

Eric cut him short, yelling, "What kind of crap is this? I've been coming here since this fucking casino opened. That's over twenty years ago. I've spent fortunes here. My film company is using several rooms right now. I'm generating a lot of business for your casino! What's the fucking problem?"

"Why are you shouting, Mr. Dagle? And I really don't appreciate your abusive language." Glugt replied quietly.

Eric responded to this rebuke by jabbing his right index finger perilously close to the casino manager's face.

"I've got a right to shout, goddammit! I'm extremely annoyed. How dare you tell me that you're cutting off my credit. Who the hell do you think you are anyway?"

Glugt waited till Eric had finished. He knew that he had the upper hand and that he wasn't going to change his mind. He was also aware that Eric had been spotted handing off chips to Peter by the 'Eye in the Sky'. These are the television cameras in the casino ceiling that monitor all the action on the floor and which are used by security on the lookout for cheaters, hustlers, thieves and other rip-off artists.

"I know who you are, Mr. Dagle," Glugt continued in a soft spoken manner. "I would like to suggest that you return to the table to play with cash or call it a night."

"I don't give a rat's ass for your fucking suggestion. I'll play when and how I want." screamed Eric, now becoming red in the face. A couple of armed security guards had appeared and taken up positions on either side of Eric, as if awaiting a development in the situation.

"What is this, the fucking Gestapo?"

With this, Glugt finally lost his patience. After giving the guards an almost imperceptible nod, the uniformed duo moved in on Eric. "Gentlemen, please escort Mr. Dagle out of the casino. He's done here."

Peter wasn't sure who made the first move because it happened so quickly. The next thing he saw was that Eric was on the floor with a guard on either side of him holding him down. He let out a wail. The guards lifted him upright by his arms and closed in on either side of his face.

"Listen buddy, you have two choices," said the more brawny of the two. "Either you walk out of here or we take you out. What's it gonna be?"

Eric grimaced in pain as he put a finger to his mouth. "I've chipped a tooth, you motherfucker! You happy now?"

Each man put a ham sized hand under Eric's shoulders and lifted him off the ground. It's a wise man who knows his own limitations and Eric eventually realized he was fighting a battle he couldn't win. He raised his hands in surrender and pulling a white handkerchief from the top pocket of his suit, he put it over his mouth and mumbled, "I'm leaving, I'm leaving, okay?"

The guards released their grip but followed closely behind him until he got to the room elevator. He pressed a button, entered and the door closed.

Peter went over to where Lucy was waiting.

"I've got to go up to give him his ten grand. Meet me at the Tiki Bar. It's over there" Peter indicating by waving his hand in the general direction. "I'll be back in ten minutes."

"You sure you want to go up there?"

"I have to. Don't leave without me."

"Okay", Lucy said resignedly. She didn't like being on her own. She could see that the bar area was populated with numerous single women waiting to be entertained. Momentarily, the thought crossed her mind that she might have made a mistake to come to Vegas but then what else could she have done. Perhaps it will work out okay, she thought as she made her way slowly to a table at the far end of the bar/restaurant trying to look as inconspicuous as possible.

Peter knocked on the door of Eric's suite.

"Just a second," Eric's voice could be heard through the door. After what seemed a long time the door opened.

"Come in."

Peter wanted to get this over as quickly as possible.

Putting the $10,000 on a mahogany leather topped desk near the window, he attempted to make light of the incident downstairs.

"At least you didn't lose any money."

"Actually, I won an extra five grand because I am not going to pay my marker back."

Peter wondered what new personality defect he had uncovered in the man that he could come out a winner but still feel that he had been a victim.

"Why?"

"Because they not only insulted and disrespected me, but I was also physically assaulted."

Peter thought of another physical assault the previous Friday. On that occasion, the victim had not been so lucky as to live to talk about it.

Eric continued; "I'm going to sue the bastards for what they did to me. Tommy is preparing a statement that she's going to release to the press tomorrow morning"

Peter thought this would be a good time to leave.

"Look, I left Lucy downstairs on her own and I've got to get back to her."

"Why didn't she come up with you?"

"She was hungry. I'm meeting her in the Chinese restaurant near the lobby." Peter lied. He was learning fast.

"Tell her to call me tomorrow morning, will you? I've got to discuss her part with her."

"Okay."

"Here," said Eric peeling off $500. "This is for you"

"Are you sure? Did I really earn it?"

"What are you talking about? A deal is a deal. I offered you 5% on my winnings, remember?"

Eric was beginning to get exasperated again.

"As I'm not going to pay my marker back after what happened to me, I started with $5,000 credit and came out with $10,000. Unless I've suddenly lost my mind, I'm well in front."

"If you say so."

"Anyway, I'm going to call it a night. God knows where I'm going to find a dentist tomorrow morning. It hurts like hell."

Peter hurried quickly down the hall and waited for the elevator. Where was Red when he needed him. Then he remembered that Red had told him that he had an important meeting and probably wouldn't see him until the following morning.

He arrived at the Tiki at a very fortuitous moment. Lucy was embroiled in a heated conversation with a man who reeked of casino security.

"What's the problem?"

"You know this lady, sir," Mr. Plainclothes asked him with a look of haughty condescension on his face.

"I most certainly do. This is Lucy Stevens and she's an actress on a movie that we are shooting in this hotel for the next five weeks. C'mon, Lucy. We're out of here."

Turning to the officious houseman, Peter remarked in a tone which could at best be described as sarcastic, "Thank you very much, officer. We appreciate your concern."

Grabbing her by her arm, Peter propelled her to the exit.

"Thank God you turned up. I had three guys come on to me."

"What, all at once?"

"Yes, almost"

"That's probably what attracted security's attention."

"Where's Red?"

"Oh, he had to see some guy. Let's get back to our hotel. I'm exhausted."

Peter may have been tired but his mind was racing. He had just witnessed another nasty side of Eric's personality. How long will it be before he became a victim of it as well? He wouldn't have long to wait.

CHAPTER 18

David Bard was not a happy man after his interview with the hotel maid, but following Patricia's disclosure of what Peter had said, his mood got even worse. The clear indication that he had been conned was still with him when he woke up Thursday morning. Not wanting to waste a minute, his first call, shortly after 8 a.m., was to Las Vegas P.D. requesting their assistance in his search for the missing witness.

No detective likes to go through the experience of being deceived by a material witness to a crime and Bard was no exception. The medicine became even more distasteful when he realized that he was going to have to do some intense police work to get the investigation back on track now that the ex-motel clerk was clearly the key to solving the crime. As he packed his bag, Bard realized that he had some unfinished business to deal with in the matter of Chester's incarceration. He could be involved in some way, he thought, let him cool his heels for the time being. He was not obliged to have him make a court appearance until Friday and if he wasn't back in Los Angeles by then, one of his deputies could deal with the matter by getting an adjournment in the legal proceedings.

Chester was transferred early on Thursday morning to the L.A. County Jail on Bauchet Street downtown with bail set at $50,000. His injured accomplice had been taken by ambulance to the jail hospital ward of the prison and his much more reasonable bail of $5,000 was due to the lack of any evidence of his having committed a serious crime.

The young blonde man had a valid California driver's license in his otherwise empty wallet under the name of Michael Booker with an address in Burbank. The paramedics had revived him just before arrival at the hospital and a report had been sent from the ward for Bard's attention along with a copy of his license.

So eager was the detective to interrogate Peter, he wanted to get to his destination as quickly as possible to track him down. On the flight to Vegas, his gut feeling told him that he was going to find him sooner rather than later.

Two uniformed officers were waiting at the airport to escort him downtown to Metro headquarters. There the special investigation detective assigned to him was waiting to be briefed on the case. It was about five p.m. when Bard finally settled into his hotel.

His Las Vegas counterparts had not been idle before his arrival. Permits for filming had to be registered with the relevant city office to be legal. Local detectives had discovered that only two feature films were being produced at that time that were in possession of the necessary authorized paperwork. One was a low budget comedy about two senior citizens having a final fling in strip clubs before moving into a home for the elderly and the other was a Mafia-oriented drama about some very unsavory characters trying to manipulate the casino gaming system.

It was not a difficult decision for Bard to go with the second of the two. He resolved to take a low profile approach by going to the listed address of the film company at Caesars Palace to do some snooping around. He didn't exactly have a lot to work with. For example, he had no idea what function Peter was fulfilling with the production nor did he know where he could be located. As darkness settled over the city, he lay on the bed in his room as he read the six page document passed on to him by LVPD.

'BLACKJACK'
'A Film By LEGITIMATE PRODUCTIONS'
Distributed by
PARAMOUNT STUDIOS.
A GULF & WESTERN COMPANY
Produced by Eric Dagle and Dan Johnson
Directed by Julio Innocente

Bard glanced only briefly at the information concerning the history behind the project and the biographies of the principal actors. He instead concentrated on the information concerning the three names on the first page, particularly the two producers, Even if they didn't know Peter personally, they possibly could put him in touch with someone who did, such as a film crew supervisor. Then he would take it from there. It seemed logical to presume that they would be staying at Caesars and he would decide what to do once he had made contact. Officially, he was obliged to observe strict inter department protocol and defer to Las Vegas P.D. in the handling of the matter in the first instance. In fact, he had made a point of accepting this but this did not prevent him from doing some reconnaissance on his own. He was very familiar with the casino from previous visits and he knew his way around.

Las Vegas is always busy but on Thursday nights the intensity increases as the weekend approaches. By the time his taxi had dropped him off outside Caesars just past the huge sign announcing Andy Williams as the resident entertainer of the week, the casino was filling up rapidly. On entering, acting on a hunch, he approached the front desk.

"Yes sir, can I help you?" inquired a mousy desk clerk who seemed to be trying to do about five things at once. Bard took out his wallet and showed him his LAPD badge.

"I'm working on a case with Las Vegas Metro and I'm hoping that I could get some assistance from you."

All of Mr. Mouse's tiny frame underneath the standard black suit, white shirt and red tie stiffened to attention. "Certainly sir. What is it you'd like to know?"

"I'm trying to locate either Mr. Eric Dagle or Mr. Dan Johnson. Could you tell me if they are registered here and if so for how long?"

"Are you here on official business, sir?" Mr. Mouse asked unnecessarily.

"You could say so, yes."

"Just for one moment I'll get the desk manager." He disappeared and came back two minutes later with an older man with black hair graying at the temples.

"I understand you need some information on a guest."

"If that's possible, yes."

Bard showed him the production document provided to him earlier. The man scanned the hotel register.

"Yes, they are both staying here. They checked in Monday night."

Pointing to a row of white phones next to the desk area, he continued, "You can call either on a house phone now if you'd like."

" I'll wait for my colleague to arrive before I do that, thank you"

"Very well, sir. Is there anything else I can do for you?"

Bard was pleased that he had made the right move and decided not to go overboard.

"No, not right now."

The somewhat unctuous manager pulled a business card out of his pocket and flipped it over before handing it to the detective with a flourish in the manner of a magician demonstrating a clever piece of sleight of hand. "Very well sir. Have a good evening."

"Oh. There's one other thing. Do you have a Peter Harris registered here?"

A slight pause while the man visited a screen invisible to his questioner.

"No, I regret that we do not."

"Okay, I was just checking."

Bard was in a hurry to move on. He found a pay phone and called Murphy, his contact on the Vegas task force. In the background at the other end of the gaming tables he could hear a male vocalist accompanied by a three piece band beginning their part of the evening's entertainment.

Murphy picked up the phone in his office just off Fremont Street downtown.

"Listen pal, I need a favor."

"Sure, what is it?"

"I tracked down those producers. Can I get one of your guys to come over with me tomorrow morning so that we can talk to at least one of them?"

"I'm glad you didn't say tonight. I've got no one available right now. We're dealing with a couple of matters that came up."

"Okay. I'll come to the station at 7:30 a.m."

"That'll work," replied Murphy enigmatically. "There'll be someone waiting for you."

CHAPTER 19

Dan had always been an easy going person. As the eldest son of the third generation of a family who had made a fortune in the pharmaceutical industry, he had enjoyed a privileged upbringing. Following a traditional Ivy League route, it was Groton to Harvard and then on to Oxford. After that straight to Wall Street following the path of his father and grandfather. However, once he became aware of the film business through a client, his interest in stocks and bonds declined precipitously. This client, a friend from the alumni association of Harvard Business School had asked him to get involved financially in a small independent film. Against all odds, it was moderately successful at the box office and Dan actually made a small profit on his investment. From that moment on it was only a matter of time that he switched from the Wall Street Journal to Variety as his first choice of daily reading matter. His relocation to California derisively described by some New Yorkers as the Coast, or even more scathingly, the Left Coast, became a formality.

This decision was very troubling to his grandfather who had seen his favorite grandson lose interest in the family business which he was being groomed to take over. He was mortified that Dan was abdicating his responsibilities just at the very time when the old man felt that the Johnson name would continue its prominence in the corporation for at least another generation. As far as Dan's father was concerned, he fully understood his son's desire to seek his own path in life but he too was desperately disappointed. Although he never spoke about it in public, something else had been troubling him about his son for some time, namely that Dan seemed to show no interest the opposite sex. He was looking forward to becoming a grandfather and although he had two daughters, Dan was his only surviving son, the other one having died tragically in an auto accident as a teenager.

Through his family background, the code of honesty and integrity remained the focal point of Dan's philosophy and his reputation of generosity to his friends was well known. After moving to Los Angeles, his Bel-Air home was the scene of many parties, lavish in their nature and where the hospitality was plentiful. Certainly it was the case that one would be hard pressed to find a person who would say anything negative about him, so distinctive a rarity in Hollywood that that in itself was a point that was constantly mentioned amongst industry insiders. Unfortunately, success and an unblemished reputation will always create jealousy in some people.

Dan met Eric at a film preview in 1975. At that time the latter had string of commercially successful B movies to his name as a producer. Eric envied Dan's ability to use his financial clout to do a lot of his talking for him. He was also astute enough to realize that from a business point of view a great deal could be achieved by forming a partnership with someone who because of this factor had the ability to make things happen. For his part, Dan admired Eric's overcoming his initial disadvantage of starting from scratch and by his sheer determination and hard work had pulled himself up by his bootlaces to the position that he had achieved within the industry. Opposites attract and this was a classic example.

It came as a considerable shock to Dan that Thursday morning in Las Vegas when Devin produced documents that indicated that the older man had been regularly siphoning off large sums of money from their joint company. He cast his mind over their long friendship in an attempt to discover if there were any tell tale signs that would have signalled Eric's fraudulent behaviour. He had been a decorated fighter pilot in the Korean war and had subsequently worked in the film industry since the late 50's. Since they began their partnership they had successfully produced four thrillers in the international espionage genre which had resulted in substantial box office receipts. What personality defect, Dan pondered, would have propelled his partner to commit blatant dishonesty which was completely contrary to the fundamental beliefs of the younger man's method of conducting business? Could the telephone message from a Los Angeles detective left on his answering service earlier that day be somehow connected?

Late on Thursday afternoon after Devin had left to return to Los Angeles, Dan got a phone call which helped to provide the answer to his self - imposed question. A senior executive at the casino was calling to ask him to come to his office as soon as possible. Politely, Dan declined as he explained that he was working in his suite and was expecting a very important phone call from California but that if the matter was urgent, he would be amenable to a visit.

"This is important. I'll come right away."

"Very well."

Dan knew better than to ask for details. A few minutes later he heard a knock on his door.

"Come in. It's open."

A man and a woman entered the room. The older of the two, a short bald man with a thick neck in his late sixties introduced himself.

"Mr. Johnson, I'm Paul Ryan head of corporate affairs at Caesars and this is my chief accountant Pauline Wallis."

"Pleased to meet you. It must be very important indeed for you both to come up here to see me."

Ryan took an envelope out of his briefcase from which he withdrew a document and gave it to Dan.

"Mr Johnson, do you recognise this banker's draft?"

Dan studied the draft carefully. It was drawn on a Paramount Studios account in the sum of $100,000. He was the beneficiary.

"No I do not."

"Look at the back of the draft; is that your signature?"

Dan turned it over and scrutinized the writing on the back of the draft carefully.

"You know, it looks like my signature, it really does but I would remember if I had signed this and I'm absolutely certain I didn't. May I ask you where you got this?"

"This draft was executed by someone claiming to be you at 7 p.m. last night in our Preferred players area."

"Excuse my ignorance, but what is a Preferred players area?"

"It's a private room on the second floor where we accommodate our clients who play for high stakes."

"Are you referring to high rollers?"

"Well, yes I am, but we don't like to call them that; we have more respect for our best customers than to use that phrase."

"Are you saying that someone received $100,000 cash from one of your employees on the strength of this draft?"

"No sir, I am not. He would have received it in the form of twenty chips of five thousand dollars each."

"And?"

Ryan's colleague interjected "We are not sure what happened next except that he didn't play for very long. We think that he may have gone downstairs shortly afterwards because later on, I regret to say he was involved in a disturbance."

"How so?"

Ryan described the circumstances, terminating the account with the revelation that Eric's public relations representative had faxed a letter to the casino threatening legal action for an assault committed on him. Throughout the conversation, neither of the casino executives had divulged that Eric was indeed the person who had cashed the draft although this was the obvious implication. Dan found this very annoying as it was obvious to him that they wanted him to set the ball rolling by accusing his partner of dishonesty rather than their making that inference in order to limit the casino's liability in any subsequent legal proceedings.

"Look, Mr. Ryan, I don't know anything about this" Dan said testily. "I'm seeing Mr. Dagle for dinner and I'll let you know if I want to take this matter any further."

"Very good; I hope you'll be in touch with us as soon as possible on this matter."

Dan noticed that Ryan had stopped calling him sir. Showing them to the door he replied "Thank you for bringing this to my attention. Good-bye."

He had remained phlegmatic and placid until the door closed behind his two visitors but privately he was seething. So Devin was right, after all. He decided he would confront Eric and demand an explanation. If the facts added up, and the evidence was as strong as it looked, Dan would make the important decision of terminating the partnership immediately on the grounds of fraud. But he would let him give his side of the story first.

CHAPTER 20

Lucy was getting ready for her dinner date with Eric when Peter called from his room. She explained on the phone that she had arranged to meet Eric in his suite at 8pm. He was trying to find a plausible reason to persuade her to postpone the appointment but he wasn't having a great deal of luck.

"Eric told me that Julio, the director is going to be joining us for dinner in one of the restaurants. I'm sure that failing to show up, and on time, would not be a good idea. Anyway this will be a good chance for me to get to know both men better. Also I want him to have a more favorable impression of me than my embarrassing performance last Friday indicated," she concluded optimistically.

Her would-be protector was in turmoil as to whether or not to reveal Eric's involvement in Catherine's death the previous Friday. If he didn't use that information to convince her to be extremely careful, he could be putting her in great personal danger. However, if he did disclose the facts, he could well be placing himself in serious jeopardy. If for some unexpected reason, Lucy exposed his part in the conspiracy to conceal a serious crime, it could lead to his being prosecuted for that offence. He decided to take another route.

"I don't have the right to tell you what to do with your life. You're the only person I've met since I arrived in Los Angeles that I have any feelings for."

"What are you trying to say?"

"Well obviously, I find you very attractive but it goes deeper than that."

"What do you mean, as deep as you went last time?"

"Oh, come on. Don't make fun of me."

In spite of himself Peter had to laugh at her bawdy sense of humour.

"I'm sorry, I just couldn't resist that. I'll let you into a little secret. I think you're not so bad yourself. I honestly believe you've created a spark in me that could lead to a future for us. How do you feel about that?"

"I'll say one thing for you," said Peter dodging the question. "You've got a lot of balls, even if you are a woman. Promise me you'll check in with me during the evening, just so that I know you are OK."

"I will, you can count on that."

" I'll see you downstairs in half an hour"

When Peter came down to the lobby, Red was waiting to drive Lucy to her rendezvous. After taking Devin to the airport, Red had picked up Dan from the film location where shooting had just about finished for the day over on Lake Las Vegas, a community about a thirty minute drive out of the city. After dropping Dan off at Caesars he had come over to the Riviera.

A weak sun was dipping out of sight with a stiff breeze picking up as he had arrived at the Riviera. In the background, diagonally across the street, the new Stratosphere Hotel arched its needle-like tower into the flat landscape that represented the back drop of downtown Las Vegas. Years earlier this area had been the hub of the action until South Las Vegas Boulevard began being the depository of the more contemporary gambling palaces that had relentlessly begun to proliferate the area.

Not being aware that Red was secretly on Dan's payroll and also not knowing if he knew of Eric's culpability in the crime, Peter instead used the time while waiting for her to join them to elaborate on the incident at David's house as his reason for wanting to keep an eye on her. As he explained it to Red, misbehavior by her would undo all the good that Dan had engendered by getting the director to agree to giving her a couple of lines in the film. So Peter asked Red for a favor.

"Could you do this for me" Peter inquired in the lobby. "Could you leave a message for me at the front desk when you know what restaurant they'll be dining in. Lucy will have her pager with so I call her on it and say that she is wanted urgently at the front desk where I will be waiting nearby. This will give her the opportunity to leave the company of the two men if she wants to."

"You think that's going to work?" Red was dubious.

"Well, she's supposed to be on the set at 6 a.m.. I'm sure she won't want to be staying up late."

The conversation was interrupted by Lucy's arrival. She was dressed to kill with a slit up the side of a black dress which also displayed a plunging neckline.

"Lucy," Peter admonished, "You're going to have dinner, not attend a world premiere."

"I know, I know, but isn't it fun?"

"Just don't lean forward. Something might fall out."

"I'll do my very breast, I mean best." Lucy chuckled.

"Save the jokes. You'll put real comedians out of business."

As the limo rolled South once again, Peter explained his plan to her. Don't worry about me so much. I can take care of myself"

Peter remained silent but wondered to himself. Am I being over protective? Would Eric do anything to hurt her? After all, this isn't motel land and Lucy's not a hooker.

Shortly after 8 p.m. Red dropped Lucy over at Caesars and took Peter across the street to the Flamingo Hotel. He had discovered that when the ten dollar phone card he had bought earlier that day was used through a hotel switchboard it lasted a much longer time than when used through a pay phone. Just another money saving device that he had been tipped off on by an operator at the Riviera, their home away from home.Peter went to the house phone and dialled the hotel operator. Explaining that it was an emergency, he asked to be put through to an L.A. number using his phone card.

"Who's this?" Patricia asked when she answered the phone.

"It's Peter. Remember I said I would call you?"

"I'm pleased to hear from you. I wasn't sure you would call"

"I don't doubt it, but I do try to keep my promises."

"How are you?"

"Well, I've had worse days. I'm glad you're still there."

"My mother went home today, but I changed my mind and I'm staying on for now."

"How long for?"

"I'm not sure. Listen, there's something you should know."

"What's that?"

"That cop is looking for you. He's real mad at you."

"Do you know why?" As if Peter didn't know already.

"Not really," she prevaricated. "But I tried to call him a couple of hours ago and the officer I spoke to at the station said he'd left town to take care of some important business connected with a suspect in my sister's death."

"Did you tell him where I was?"

Patricia was evasive.

"I mentioned that you'd called me from an airport phone. You know, we didn't speak for very long. Can you talk right now? I was hoping you'd tell me more about what happened to my sister."

"There's not a lot more that I can say except that I'm responsible for her being in the room with the guy and he disappeared after your sister died. I'm very sorry that I was ever involved in this; I've never had anything like this happen to me before."

:"What are you going to do now?"

"I don't have many options, do I? I was hoping that I could find a way out of this mess but I'm not being very realistic. I'll turn myself in when I get back to Los Angeles if Bard doesn't find me first. He's probably here looking for me right now."

"Don't you have anything else you want to say to me?"

"I hope I've convinced you I had nothing to do with your sister's death."

"I believe you. But please call me again tomorrow and let me know when you are coming back. I can't stay here forever"

"Ok I'll call you tomorrow same time. Bye"

At exactly the same time Peter was having this conversation, an important meeting was taking place in the executive offices at Caesars. To put it mildly, Ryan had been extremely disappointed at the reaction of Dan Johnson's after he had acknowledged that his signature had been forged to cash a banker's draft for such a large sum of money. Hell, thought Ryan, if someone tried to steal ten dollars from me I'd be pissed. He informed his three fellow executives with him at the meeting that he intended to file a criminal complaint the next morning with Las Vegas police against Eric Dagle. The guy must have had a colossal nerve, Ryan declared to his colleagues. He's threatening to sue us for cutting off his credit line having the very same evening defrauded us of $100,000. He thought he'd experienced every casino con artist that existed. From the chip stealers to the purse and wallet snatchers, even the roulette slot wideners and the scammers who used an electronic device to get the machines to cough up quarters, not to mention the jokers who stuck thin wires in the coin slots. But this was an operation of a much more sophisticated type which had to be taken care of with maximum response. Furthermore, Mr. Dagle would be informed at the same time that his presence on the premises was no longer acceptable and that he would need to find alternative accommodation in the city immediately. As far as that was concerned, a jail cell would be most appropriate, Ryan concluded.

Blissfully unaware of this development, Dan called Devin upon his return to Los Angeles and informed him that Eric had apparently cashed a $100,000 draft at Caesars by forging his signature.

Devin strongly advised him to wait until his return the following day at noon so they could confront Eric together with the evidence.

Amazingly, Eric was behaving that evening as if he didn't have a care in the world. On arrival at Caesars, Lucy called Eric's suite from the lobby. Eric explained that he was having a meeting with Tommy and Julio was on his way over to go though some script alterations with him. He suggested she come up to his suite where they could go over her lines before the director arrived. Then they would all go for dinner in a hotel restaurant. Lucy thought this was a good idea. As she went up in elevator she checked herself in the mirror. She arrived at the suite on the eighteenth floor and knocked on the door.

"Come in. Come in. The door's open."

Eric rose from a leather couch in the living room and greeted her warmly. He was dressed in an immaculately cut blue suit and looked ready to go out for the evening. Tommy waved her welcome from her seat behind a desk in a corner of the room where she appeared to be having an intense conversation on the telephone.

"Sit down, make yourself comfortable. What would you like to drink?"

"I don't mind. Whatever you suggest." Lucy replied candidly.

"I'll take care of it. Julio should be here very soon. Have you heard from Peter?"

"I don't know where he is right now; he was with Red earlier when he dropped me off. "

"You look great. I'm sure Julio will be very impressed."

What Lucy didn't know was that when Red had called a little earlier to find out where they were going to dine that evening using the excuse that he would like to know in case his services were needed later, Eric had informed him that he was going to remain in his suite and have dinner served there.

Needless to say, Red digested this development with grave misgivings. He had to decide quickly what he needed to do. Using the car phone he called Caesars and left a message for Peter to call him immediately.

After having a drink in the bar at the Flamingo, Peter decided to call Caesars and was given Red's message. On the follow up call to the car, the information he was given struck him like a thunderbolt.

Pushing his way through the Flamingo's customers and expending even further time getting across the exceptionally crowded street, he hurried up the long driveway of Caesars. Peter sprinted past the fountains and rushed through a long line of taxis waiting to pick up their passengers.

In the meantime, Red, realizing that Peter had a problem with Lucy being in close quarters with Eric for whatever reason, decided that he would inform Dan where he was headed. There's safety in numbers, Red thought as he negotiated the heavy night traffic on the Strip.

As Peter fought his way through the casino floor, the rows of slot machines were noisily ingesting coins as greedily as they were being pumped in by a multitude of gamblers. As he swept by, Peter was struck by what he had been told was the futility of gambling on slots. Las Vegas casinos loftily claimed that at least 95% of the coins invested were returned to the gambler, but any mathematician worth his salt could, he realized, readily deduce that that remaining 5% profit gradually becomes a law of diminishing returns. If a customer played the slots for long enough they would eventually lose all of their money unless they were one of the small fraction who were incredibly lucky. A friendly bellman at the Riv, as Peter's temporary home was known locally, had related with some degree of scorn the story of daily busloads of lowly paid visitors from California. These people would spend ten hours on the road to and from Vegas, sometimes with less than a hundred dollars to play the machines and often lost everything in less than half an hour.

Peter looked at his watch. It was a good idea to have purchased another one after getting his first week's pay, particularly on this occasion, as clocks don't exist in Las Vegas casinos for an obvious reason. It was ten past nine. He elbowed his way through the crowd watching a football playoff game just outside the Racebook. He was about to turn the corner to the carpeted pathway leading to the bank of elevators, when he felt a hand firmly grasp his left arm.

"Hello smart ass. I've been looking for you." It was Bard.

Peter swallowed hard. Although he was frantic in his desire to get to Eric's suite, he tried to remain calm.

"Hi."

"You don't seem very surprised to see me."

"No, detective. I'm not surprised at all. Patricia Mack told me you were probably on your way here when I spoke to her earlier this evening. Believe it or not, I'm glad to see you."

Peter could not believe he was speaking in such a composed manner to the one man who controlled his immediate future so decisively.

"We have to go into a casino office where I need to question you."

"Please don't do this to me now, I beg you. You don't know how important it is for me to be somewhere upstairs right away."

Bard stiffened.

"Listen fella, you don't have much choice. Right now I've got a probable cause case against you and if you give me any trouble, I'll just drop all the small talk and turn you into the locals pronto. Is that what you want?"

"Okay, you win. "

Peter decided to stall for time knowing very well that he was headed for a police station anyway. He walked in tandem with Bard across a sloping walkway dividing the two casino sections and as the detective turned right to go past a coffee shop, he saw his chance. A group of elderly matrons were in line waiting to enter and as Bard hesitated to allow four of them to go in together, Peter suddenly turned on his heels and dashed off in the opposite direction back toward the elevators.

Swearing loudly, Bard tried to plow through the group of women and at the same time keep from losing sight of Peter. Running through any part of a Las Vegas casino immediately attracts the attention of a security patrol and this instance was no exception. A uniformed guard took up the chase as well but somehow Peter managed to evade him also and get into an elevator. The door closed behind him before either pursuer could catch up.

The sign above the door indicated that Peter was going to the eighteenth floor and Bard and the security officer jumped into an adjacent elevator. While they were ascending, the detective rapidly explained the circumstances of his pursuit.

To his surprise, when the doors opened, Peter was waiting for them.

"Look, this is crazy but you've got to believe me," Peter spoke in overdrive. "The guy responsible for the death at the motel is in suite 1869 and he's got another girl who's a friend of mine in there with him. We've got to get her out before anything happens to her. I swear I'm not making this up. I know it looks bad that I ran away but she's in great danger."

"Do I cuff him?" the guard asked Bard.

Bard replied quickly.

"You bet your life. I'm not going to take the chance of this joker giving me the slip again."

"It's down this way," Peter gestured with his shackled hands, pointing to the numbered signs on the wall. "Hurry!"

When they arrived at the suite, Bard knocked hard on the door.

Silence.

"Have you got a pass key?"

"Yes, I am head of security on this shift"

"Open it"

Turning to Peter. "If this is a fucking joke, you're in even worse trouble."

The guard put his key in the door and opened it.

They noticed immediately that the suite had a living room with a desk, chairs and a large couch with cushions. Beyond the couch was a closed door which presumably led to a bedroom.

Bard knocked on the door. "Is anyone in there?" he yelled while the guard was on his radio alerting his superiors of the situation. The detective went into the kitchen to rummage through the drawers looking for something to force the door. Suddenly it opened and Eric appeared. His face was contorted with rage.

"What the hell do you think you're doing?" he screamed at Bard.

Bard replied matter-of-factly "Are you Eric Dagle?"

"Yes."

"Do you have a young lady in there with you, sir?"

"No I don't but even if I did, what business is it of yours? Who are you anyway?'

Suddenly Eric noticed Peter who had been keeping out of sight.

"Are you the reason for all this commotion, Peter?"

Bard put his hand up to stop Peter replying.

"Just calm down sir and I will explain everything" said the detective, showing his badge.

Eric continued to stand defiantly in the doorway to the bedroom, with his arms crossed. It was then that Peter decided to disobey Bard by entering the conversation.

"Eric, Lucy called me half an hour ago to say she was here with you," he lied.

"Well, Peter, your story doesn't seem to be believed judging by the fact that you look like you're under arrest."

The security guard interceded.

"Sir, we have the right to look around your suite to check things out. We'd like to do that now if you'll kindly move to one side."

"If you insist, but there's nobody here."

Eric had thought very quickly when he heard the loud banging on the door. Lucy had passed out several minutes earlier after finishing the spiked drink that she had accepted from Eric. He had carried her into the bedroom and was in the process of undressing her on the bed when he was interrupted by the commotion outside. Thinking quickly, he realised there was enough space in the closet to accommodate her unconscious body. Bundling her into the enclosed space, he closed the door and locked it, putting the key in his pocket and smoothed the comforter down on the bed before opening the door to his uninvited visitors.

Bard tried to stop Peter from coming into the bedroom with them, but he pushed his way in anyway. While Eric stood quietly to one side, the men looked around. The guard took a brief look under the bed. Bard motioned toward the closet.

"What's in there?"

"That's a door leading to the next suite. I don't have a key for it."

After Bard inspected the door he was about to leave the bedroom with Peter following reluctantly behind. As the latter was leaving the room he gave one last look round. Suddenly, he spotted it. A small purse was lying almost out of sight underneath the divan.

"Hey!" Peter shouted. "Look at that.!"

The three men turned around and stood quite still as if waiting for Eric to provide an explanation. There was a moment of silence that seemed to last for an eternity as the detective and Eric eyeballed each other.

"Well...." Bard began, and paused, waiting for Eric's response to this dramatic development.

"One of my guests here earlier must have left it behind.. I'll just-

Bard interrupted. "Don't touch it." he barked. "Stand over there and don't move."

The guard picked up the small purse and attempted to hand it to Bard who waved him off.

"You take a look for I.D.. inside. I'm not officially authorized to handle evidence unless LVPD is present."

The security officer opened the purse and pulled out a small leather wallet. Inside the wallet was some cash, a couple of business cards and California I.D.

He scrutinized the name on the card.

"Lucy Stevens." he said aloud.

Peter was about to say something but Bard silenced him with a raised finger and gave him a stern look.

"How do you respond to the fact that this wallet obviously belongs to the young lady allegedly asked by this young man" pointing to Peter "to meet her here in your suite." he inquired of Eric.

"I have a suggestion. If you will allow me to call my publicity chief who is staying here on the 17th floor and who left here 15 minutes ago, she will tell you that we have been talking together here for the previous hour and a half and there was no one else here during that time," volunteered Eric.

"That won't be necessary" replied Bard. "We will wait for local officers to arrive."

"And what happens then?"

"That depends on them," replied Bard. "I need to use the phone.

Where is it?"

"It's over there," said Eric pointing to a table alongside the bed.

After contacting Murphy downtown, requesting assistance, Bard asked casually "Where's your bathroom?"

He crossed the bedroom and turned left in the direction of Eric's pointing finger. Satisfied that there was no one there, he returned to face the producer.

"You may need a coat, it's getting chilly out there. Okay, this is what is going to happen. We're going to wait here until LVPD arrive. In the meantime you might want to avail yourself of the opportunity to tell me what you know about an incident at a motel in Hollywood on Friday which I'm investigating."

"I don't know what you're talking about."

"Very well. One thing's for sure; you say that the young lady who we're looking for and whose purse we've just found in your bedroom has not been here, while Peter over here says the woman whose ID is in this purse contacted him to say she was in your suite. So, one of you is lying, right?"

"Well, it's not me" said Eric petulantly.

"We'll see about that."

Bard was interrupted by a knock on the door. Ryan the casino chief and a younger man who was built like an NFL blocker entered the suite.

"We just got a call from security. What's going on here?" asked Ryan.

Briefed by Bard, he showed no emotion but nodded his head slowly.

Finally he spoke.

"It gets better or worse depending on which way you look at it. Can I have a word with you in private?" Bard nodded and gestured to the guard, pointing at Eric, "Keep an eye on him."

He closed the door of the bedroom and followed Ryan and his companion and into the living room. After about five minutes, he came back without the other two who had left to wait for the police by the elevators.

"It looks bad Eric, real bad."

"What do you mean?" asked Eric hesitantly obviously concerned that the emphasis of the investigation had shifted even more in his direction.

"What I mean is you're going to need more than a coat. How about a toothbrush."

"Can I tell my publicist where I'm going?"

"You've got thirty seconds. By the way, where do you keep your clothes. You know, like suits, shirts and shoes?

Eric ignored the question and went to the telephone on a table next to the bed. Suddenly in a swift move he jerked open the drawer, reached in with his right hand and pulled out a black automatic. Pointing it at the guard who had remained in the room with Bard and Peter, he shouted "Take off your gun belt and throw it over here. Now!"

The guard complied.

"I don't want to shoot any of you but I will if you do anything stupid."

"Don't be ridiculous" said Bard quietly. "You won't get anywhere with this attitude."

Eric ignored him and motioned to the guard while taking a key out of his left trouser pocket with his other hand.

"Come over here and open this door behind me with the key and bring out the woman who's in there. So now you know, don't you?" He sneered at Bard. Eric shifted slightly as he tossed the key to the guard while keeping his eyes and his gun trained on the other two men.

"Slowly now, very slowly." he commanded the officer. The man opened the door of what he had claimed was the connection to the next suite. The unconscious figure of Lucy was slumped on the floor.

"Put her on the bed and get down on the floor on your stomach.," Eric demanded. "All of you! Spread your legs. You too, detective."

After seeing the men comply, Eric edged slowly to the bed and lifted Lucy with his left arm into a standing position with her body between himself and the others.

"I mean this very seriously. One false move and the girl gets a bullet in the head."

Slowly, Eric edged past the prone threesome towards the door leading to the living room with the muzzle of his gun resting on Lucy's temple. Concentrating on Bard and the security guard, he failed to see that Peter had stretched his hands out in front of him as far as possible. As he edged passed Peter, the chance came and he took it. When Eric lifted his right foot off the ground, Peter slipped the handcuffs under it and gave his leg a powerful tug.

Startled and off balance, Eric stumbled and fell over backwards. As the guard scrambled for his gun, Eric instantly aimed toward him and fired two shots. The other man fell back mortally wounded.

The third round Eric saved for himself. He pointed the gun at his right temple and pulled the trigger. Blood splattered on the wall behind him as Ryan and his colleague rushed into the room.

CHAPTER 21

The flight back to LAX late on Friday morning lasted less than an hour but to Peter it seemed like an eternity. Bard had to get back to make the court appearance in Chester's case and he wasn't going to leave without his chief witness. He made arrangements to return to Vegas on Sunday to finish the important paperwork related to Eric's criminal activity at Caesars.

"That guy saved us a lot of problems by blowing himself away" said Murphy at the airport where he had escorted the two men. Lucy was expected to be discharged that afternoon from the hospital where she had been undergoing a comprehensive check up and was due to go back to Los Angeles later that evening escorted by Red.

"We would've had to charge him with Murder in the first degree not to mention the messy business over the casino fraud," continued Murphy. "Who knows how long that trial would have taken. Get the photo?"

"Yeah, it would have been a pain," retorted Bard. "The jury system is the price we pay for democracy."

"I'll see you when you get back. Obviously it'd help to have your friends at the inquest. We probably won't get a lot of cooperation from that dyke publicist as we are charging her with being an accomplice with the attack on the girl," concluded the Vegas detective wearily.

As for the shooting schedule on the film, a decision was made by Dan early on Friday to halt production for seven days although all cast and crew

189

would be paid in full in the interim by the insurance company. The press and television outlets locally and later on that afternoon and evening in Los Angeles had a field day with the story. Eric's body was taken to the morgue downtown and would remain there until the funeral arrangements were made. The memorial service and the burial for the unfortunate security guard would take place the following Tuesday. When Devin came back to Vegas on Friday afternoon, he was immediately pressed into service by Dan to take care of all the details as well as brief the company's employees on the developments.

On their arrival in Los Angeles, a black and white was waiting for Bard and Peter was put into the back for their trip to Hollywood. He expected to be remanded in custody until bail was set and probably after that as well as he was unable to think of anyone who would come up with the cash bond needed to release him. The owners of the two bail bond offices on the other side of the street from the police station on Wilcox were more than likely to be reluctant to consider helping someone who had already resisted arrest.

The police car entered the garage at the back of the station and Bard got out from the front passenger seat to take Peter inside the building. He was led down a hallway at the end of which was a dimly lit room to the right. His escort motioned to him to sit down at a chair by a desk which was cluttered with papers.

Bard got straight to the point.

"Peter, you've been a bad boy. You caused me a lot of problems."

"You're right, I'm sorry."

Bard lit a cigarette and blew the smoke towards the closed window which overlooked the courtyard. Peter followed the direction of the smoke and looked out the window at the police wagons specially designed to hold several prisoners at one time. He had observed the spectacle on many previous occasions when he had happened to be on Sunset late at night. There were so many prostitutes plying their trade until 7 a.m. or even later on the stretch of the Boulevard between Fairfax and Western that the police procedure in these situations resembled the exercise of shooting fish in a barrel. 'Girlfriend, paddywagon coming!' was the familiar refrain of warning as the women scattered like rats down a hole when the black van came into view in the cat and mouse operation.

"I did a bad thing," Peter continued. "I got tempted but as soon as I realized the implications involved, I began to feel guilty and things went rapidly downhill from there."

Bard looked at Peter for what seemed like a full minute before responding. "I can see how you got sucked in. That guy was a real Jekyll and Hyde character and the evil part of him was very severe. He was going to be arrested in a few hours for check fraud anyway so his future didn't look good. The problem I have with you is that you've committed a criminal offense and I have to find a way to resolve this."

Bard paused as if mentally trying to find a solution.

"This might work. There's a guy down at County who I've got to charge on the motel matter or release him. You know who I'm talking about, don't you?"

191

Peter nodded as Bard continued. "Yes, I thought you might remember Chester, the guy you tried to stick for the homicide in room 210. Well, he's not feeling too happy right now as you can well imagine You would be a great help to us both by coming to the jail now and apologising for trying to frame him for the crime. That's after making a statement on the record about what really happened and signing it." What Bard didn't add was that this would help straighten out some details of Chester's imprisonment on Wednesday, especially as far as the detective's liability was concerned.

Peter hesitated before responding to this overture. The detective read his mind right away.

"I know what you're thinking. Well obviously, I'm going to take into consideration that you got us out of a big jam at Caesars by your quick thinking but I'm not going to let you off the hook completely."

Peter shrugged his shoulders.

"I guess I don't have a choice."

"That's perfectly correct. You don't."

While he was completing his statement, there was a knock on the door.

Lopez entered the room.

"Hey lieutenant, we got the bail for the other guy in the car with Chester covered by a man who came into the station. Should we have waited for you to speak to him?"

"Not really. I'm glad you dealt with it. Who was he anyway?"

"Said he's a doctor. He gave us two pieces of ID which looked pretty legit and paid in cash. As far as we know, his friend's still pretty banged up at County in the hospital ward"

The trip downtown took less than half an hour. On the way down, Bard reflected on a statement that he once read that Harvey Keitel made to Marty Scorsese on the set of Taxi Driver when he was rationalizing his role. "There is great humanity in a pimp, humanity in its suffering sense. They come out of a place of great need, usually of poverty, of broken homes, of never having opportunity." Bard was pretty sure he didn't agree with that sentiment.

The Bauchet Street hotel accommodation is a grim building occupying two full blocks opposite the now empty Los Angeles river basin. The detective was escorted with his companion to Chester's cell.

"Hey Chester, how ya doing?"

Chester looked as if he had lost a hundred dollars and found a dime. "Not too good right now, my face is still hurting me."

Bard ignored Chester's doleful remark.

"Well buddy, this is your lucky night. I've talked with our motel clerk here and it looks like we're going to spring you. Remember your young friend?" gesturing to Peter. "He has something to say to you."

"That's right, Chester, I told the detective that you had nothing to do with what happened on Friday. I'm responsible for getting you into this mess and I'm sorry."

Bard waited awhile for the prisoner to absorb this development before continuing.

"Guess what that means now, Chester?"

"Are you dropping the charges?"

"That's right. I'm going to pass on your evading arrest on Wednesday. Once you sign a piece of paper saying that you don't intend to sue us for infringing on your constitutional rights, I'm willing to release you. What've you got to say to that?"

"Hey man, better late than never. Can my friend be released too?"

"Oh he got bail already but he's too hurt to move right now."

"Can I see him?"

"He's in another area, but we can check on him on the way out. I'm not sure that he knows that he got bailed out by a friend."

Bard motioned to the jailer to unlock the cell door. Inside the latter's office, Chester completed the paperwork and followed the other two across the landing into the hospital area. The detective consulted the wall chart at the entrance for the name and bed number. Walking into the ward, he paused at the fourth bed on the right. Looking at the dozing prisoner, Bard shook the cot slightly.

"Hey, wake up guy, your friend's here to see you."

The occupant of the bed turned over to face his visitors. He was an Oriental - Chester's associate was no longer in the ward. The jailer was momentarily puzzled, but quickly regained his memory.

"That's right - when I came on duty just before you got here, I was told that he got loaded into a Parkway ambulance by two paramedics and left about an hour ago after signing a release form. Once we were told by Wilcox he had made bail we had no legal right to detain him any longer"

Peter followed Chester and Bard into the car park. A light drizzle had begun to fall. Chester waited at the back door of Bard's vehicle to be let in, taking it for granted that he would be accompanying the other two back to Hollywood but the detective had other plans.

"You know, Chester I have a sinking feeling that you and your friend are involved in some shady business and I'm sure we're gonna meet again. My gut feeling tells me I should take you back into custody but that would mean I'd be breaking my word, so we're parting company right here....for now."

"You mean I can't get a ride with you guys?"

"Nope, this is it. It's time for you to get a better life and that time starts right now. Adios amigo."

Fat chance, Bard thought as he watched Chester trudge off on foot towards Union Station. After he got on the 101 freeway to return to Hollywood, he got a call from Wilcox. Officer Hernandez was on the line. Patricia had called in asking to see him as soon as possible.

"That doctor who went bail, what's his name and address,?" Bard asked. Peter was stunned when he repeated the name. He never even considered thinking that Doctor Domi, as Dan called him, would be involved with such a low-life character. After expressing his amazement at this development to Bard, the latter asked. "You don't know Chester's friend, do you?"

Bard passed the copy of the released driver's license to Peter. The latter gasped at the sight of the mug shot.

It was T-shirt!

The detective took the surprise news with a shrug of his shoulders.

"Let's go check out the quack right away. He could be a dealer. That would be a bundle of laughs, wouldn't it?"

* * * * *

The entrance to Dan's estate was open which astonished Peter. Bard drove through the gates and switched his lights off before they reached the mansion which was in darkness. He parked the car and the two men continued on foot. By now the light had faded completely although the sky was clear. On the way up they had noticed a cottage on the left of the main residence which appeared to be inhabited, with lights on in the rear casting a glow toward which they now advanced. As they got closer, the sound of conversation became clear. The detective put his finger to his lips and beckoned to Peter to follow him around to the other side of the bungalow. Looking though a window, Peter saw Dr. Domi lying on a couch with his companion sitting across from him rubbing his nose. On the table between them, was a silver bowl full of what appeared to be cocaine between two small mirrors. As the blonde man leaned forward to scoop out some of the powder onto one of the mirrors, Bard pointed at him and looked at Peter with a quizzical expression on his face.

"Is that him?" he whispered.

Peter nodded.

Bard motioned to Peter to follow him back towards his car. The detective picked up his phone and called Wilcox. Satisfied that Lopez and his partner were on their way, Bard drove back down to the entrance and took an orange cone out of the trunk of his vehicle and placed it on the sidewalk for his officers' guidance, as he had arranged with them. He had just returned to his original parking place on the property, when he heard the sound of a car making a turn into the driveway. A dark limousine swept by and Bard could see by its lights that it had come to a stop at the top of the hill.

Moving swiftly, the two men returned to the bungalow in time to see Dan approaching it from the rear. Bard and Peter followed closely. The producer climbed the steps and entered the small living room. The doctor's guest looked up in surprise.

"Hi. We didn't expect you back this weekend. What's going on?"

"What do you mean by 'what's going on'. Haven't you heard the news?"

"No man, I don't watch much TV. Anyway, I've been out of commission the last couple of days."

"Well, it doesn't matter right now. Why are you here exactly?"

"Oh, I'm just visiting Domi. We're good friends."

"I know who you are and I don't like you."

Turning to Domi who appeared to be unresponsive, "I need to talk to you. You have to get your friend out of here."

The doctor's only acknowledgement of Dan's remarks was to nod his head slightly.

"Can you hear me? Time to wake up!" Dan went across to the couch and put his hand underneath Dominick's head in an effort to get a response.

"Hey man, leave him alone. He's just resting after a long day."

Dan's expressionless face now turned into a scowl.

"I've heard enough from you. Get out of my house now."

"This isn't your house and I'm not leaving. Chill out, man."

Dan leaped across the room and grabbed the younger man by the arm and began to pull him towards the door. T-shirt grappled with the older man and threw him on the floor. As he tried to get up, his attacker picked up a wine bottle from a table and was about to hit him with it when Bard who had witnessed the unfolding drama hurled himself through the door with his automatic in his right hand.

"That's enough from you guy, I'm a police officer. Put your hands up. Go and lean against the wall."

Peter went over to Dan and helped him into a chair. Turning to T-shirt, he asked, "Remember me? Three weeks ago in that apartment in Hollywood?"

T-shirt turned sideways to look at Peter as Bard was putting the cuffs around his wrists behind his back.

"I've never seen you before in my life."

"Oh yes you have."

Bard intervened. "Is your name Michael Booker?"

"Yes it is."

"You're under arrest on suspicion of assault and battery on this gentleman at a residence in Hollywood and of causing actual bodily harm to the owner of this property five minutes ago in this room."

Bard took his suspect through the doorway and down the steps to the black and white which had just pulled up outside. The two officers got out of the vehicle and approached.

"Hey lieutenant, what we got here?"

"Put him in the back. I'm not done here yet."

The detective went back into the bungalow and joined the other three. Looking at Dan, he came straight to the point.

"What is your connection with this man, exactly?" pointing to the doctor.

"He's my very close friend who happens to live in this cottage with my permission."

"Do you know he bailed out this guy earlier today from prison – this same guy who just tried to kill you?"

Dan put his head in his hands. "Jesus, no I did not."

"Do I have your permission to look around this place?"

"Why would you want to do that?"

"I've got a feeling that there's a lot more illegal substances here than this," pointing to the cocaine on the table. "I could get a search warrant but that's going take some time and I'd like your cooperation. Anyway, I'm taking this with me as evidence when I leave."

"I'm not sure I want you to turn this place over. I'll need to consult my lawyer."

"As you wish. You know something, your friend over here doesn't look too good. He hasn't said a word since we've been here. I think I'll call an ambulance for him right now."

Dan failed to respond so Bard took the questioning up a notch.

"Are you in a relationship with this man?"

"That's really none of your business. I don't have to answer that."

"Very well, but I have a feeling that you're going have to do exactly that sooner rather then later."

Bard turned to Lopez who had come into the room during the conversation. "Get an ambulance up here, pronto."

"Okay, Lieutenant."

Motioning to Dan, the detective got straight to the point. "I'd like a statement from you so I need you to come back with me to the station after the ambulance arrives. In the meantime, I suggest you stay here with Peter and try to help your friend. Was anyone else with you in the limo?"

"Yes, that would be Red, my driver. He's up at the house. Is it okay if he stays there? I need someone to look after the place until I get back," Dan responded in a more contrite manner.

Bard was unresponsive and instead went outside to talk to his officers.

"Okay you guys can take our man to Hollywood and book him. I'll get down as quickly as I can after the ambulance gets here."

"You got it, Lieutenant."

When the ambulance had taken the doctor to Hollywood Presbyterian Hospital, Bard returned to the police station with Peter where they found Patricia waiting for him just outside his office. The detective showed her his sympathetic side.

"Well, we got the bad guy, you'll be pleased to hear, with a certain amount of help from this young man," nodding at Peter, "Unfortunately, he won't be around to tell us why he was such an asshole, if you pardon my language."

"The Sergeant here gave me some of the details. I'm very relieved to know its over," responded the young woman. "Thank you very much. I've already told my mother and she thanks you too."

"Would you ask her to give me a call tomorrow? I'd like to speak to her personally." Turning to Peter, "Why don't you take this young lady back to her motel? I'll provide a car for the journey but I have to stay here to get on with my paperwork. I'll need you later so don't disappear again."

"You mean I'm free to go for now?"

"Well, I'm going to need you as a witness against Mr. Booker so we have to discuss that by tomorrow afternoon, at the latest. I suggest you check back into your lodgings so I know where to find you and this time, don't leave town."

"Thanks for going easy on me."

"I'm not going easy on you. I warn you right now if you do something stupid I'll hunt you down and when I find you I'll lock you up and throw the key away. You can take that to the bank."

Hernandez came in to the room while Bard was talking. "Hey, Lieutenant, we just got word from the paramedics. The doc didn't make it. He was D O A when they got him to the hospital."

The couple were leaving the station together when Red pulled up at the entrance in the limo. The window on the passenger side at the rear rolled down and Lucy stuck her head out.

"I just had to come and see you right away when I heard you were here to thank you for saving my life."

"It's nice to know that I finally managed to do something right," said Peter sheepishly.

"Call me." With that, she threw Peter a kiss. As window rolled up, Peter recognised the profile of

Devin sitting close to her with his arm around her shoulder. While waiting for the police that was coming to pick Patricia and himself up, Peter noticed T-shirt being escorted to a black and white to be taken downtown. As he got in, their eyes met. Peter couldn't resist the temptation:

"Welcome to Hollywood!"

* * * * *

"CUT!! That's a wrap." said Eric as he climbed off his chair to a thunderous round of applause from the location crew.

"I'm happy with that shot, how about you guys?" gesturing to the camera man and his assistant.

"Looks good to me," answered the cinematographer

"I'm fine with that too", chimed in 'Bard'.

"How about you two?" gestured the director to 'Peter' and 'Lucy' who were holding hands at the side of the set. Before he could get a response, the actor portraying the detective interjected again:

"Hey Eric. The next movie we do together, make sure I get the girl!"

The author has been a resident of Los Angeles for over 25 years and has covered the Hollywood scene extensively as a writer and a journalist. During that period, he has been fortunate enough to meet, and in many cases, have extensive conversations with a high percentage of the major players, both behind and in front of the camera. For his next project, he is researching a novel based on the American horse-racing industry, which will include an emphasis on gambling issues.